Memoirs of a Geisha

ARTHUR GOLDEN

Level 6

Retold by Michael Dean
Series Editors: Andy Hopkins and Jocelyn Potter

Pearson Education Limited

Edinburgh Gate, Harlow,
Essex CM20 2JE, England
and Associated Companies throughout the world.

ISBN: 978-1-4058-8267-5

First published in the UK by Chatto and Windus, one of the
publishers in the Random House Group Ltd. 1997
New edition first published by Penguin Books Ltd 2000
This edition first published 2008

3

Typeset by Graphicraft Ltd, Hong Kong
Set in 11/14pt Bembo
Printed in China
SWTC/03

Published by Pearson Education Ltd

Every effort has been made to trace the copyright holders and we apologise in advance
for any unintentional omissions. We would be pleased to insert the appropriate
acknowledgement in any subsequent edition of this publication.

For a complete list of the titles available in the Pearson English Readers series, please
visit www.pearsonenglishreaders.com. Alternatively, write to your local Pearson Education
office or to Pearson English Readers Marketing Department, Pearson Education,
Edinburgh Gate, Harlow, Essex CM20 2JE, England.

Contents

Introduction

"But Mameha-san, I don't want kindness!"

"Don't you? I thought we all wanted kindness. Maybe what you mean is that you want something more than kindness. And that is something you're in no position to ask for."

It is New York, in 1985. A Professor of Japanese History, Jakob Haarhuis, has persuaded an old Japanese woman to tell him the story of her life. The old woman eventually agrees, and what you will read here is the unforgettable result: *Memoirs of a Geisha*. In this story you will follow Nitta Sayuri on an unbelievable journey, from her early years as a child in a small fishing village, through her time as a great geisha in the golden age of Gion, the geisha area of Kyoto, to her old age in New York.

Memoirs of a Geisha is set against the background of what the Japanese call *kuraitani*—the valley of darkness; the terrible years of the economic Depression of the 1930s and, later, World War II. It is one woman's story of survival in a hard world where men have all the power and women are expected to be nothing more than beautiful toys. Sayuri suffers greatly at the hands of Hatsumomo, a beautiful but evil geisha who is determined that Sayuri will spend the rest of her life as a humble maid. Sayuri is cruelly and unjustly treated until one day another geisha, Mameha, mysteriously enters her life and helps her in her war against Hatsumomo.

This is not, however, only a story of a woman's survival. It is also the story of her refusal to give up her secret love for a man who once offered her a small sign of kindness. This man is one of the most important men in Kyoto, and seems completely out of reach, but Sayuri never loses her love for him, and is determined never to betray her heart. This determination, however, leads to a complex moral and emotional problem. If she wishes to become a geisha, Sayuri needs somehow to defeat Hatsumomo. But what happens if the only way to defeat Hatsumomo involves losing, forever, the chance of being with the man she loves? This struggle between the need to survive and the need for love is the central issue in Sayuri's life and provides the dramatic heart of her fascinating story. It leads to many heart-breaking situations, which Sayuri learns to handle with a calm bravery. However, as her power in the geisha world gradually increases, the object of her heart's desire still remains as out of reach as ever. She becomes desperate, but never loses hope, and we see another, more calculating, side of her character. We may not agree with everything that Sayuri has to do to achieve her dream, but she never loses our sympathy. In a cruel, unforgiving world, survival is considered the only success and love is thought of as an unobtainable luxury. Sayuri disagrees, and it is the description of her search for both that gives this story its power and beauty, and makes *Memoirs of a Geisha* one of the great stories of our time.

One of the interesting features of this story is the detailed description of the different stages that a girl must pass through in order to become a geisha. Many people believe that part of a geisha's work involves having paid sex with their clients, but this is untrue. Geisha are traditional female Japanese entertainers whose skills include conversation; playing Japanese instruments such as the *shamisen* (Japanese guitar) or *tsutsumi* (a small drum); the famous tea ceremony, and formal dance. Their appearance is also very important, and geisha usually have professional assistants to help them put on their clothes. They have to wear several layers of *kimono* (a loose piece of clothing with wide sleeves), and their *obi* (belt) is more than a simple band of cloth. Sayuri describes how heavy and difficult to wear these clothes are when she is training to be a novice. A novice's *obi* is much longer than the one that older people wear—it can stretch from "one end of a room to the other." All geisha need help with their *obis* because they have to be tied at the back (unlike women who have sex with their clients, who tie their *obis* at the front).

Sayuri also describes having her hair done as the first step to being a novice. The process is so complicated that geisha dare not sleep on an ordinary pillow afterwards—they have to sleep with a special pillow (a *takamakura*) under their necks.

In the 1920s, when this story takes place, there were over 80,000 geisha in Japan. Today, however, there are very few. It has been estimated that there are between one thousand and two thousand geisha in modern Japan. Kyoto (where Sayuri's story takes place) is the city where the geisha tradition is the strongest today. One reason for the gradual disappearance of geisha in modern-day Japan is the decline of interest in traditional arts. Many of the activities and traditions described in the story are much rarer today. For example, much of the story in *Memoirs of a Geisha* centers around Sayuri's search for a *danna* (a wealthy man who will provide for her financially on a long-term basis). A visitor to Japan today can still see geisha in the street, but these "geisha" are often tourists who have paid to be dressed up as one!

The writer of this story, Arthur Golden, was born in Chattanooga, Tennessee, in the United States. He studied at Harvard and Boston Universities and worked on a magazine in Japan before returning to the United States. He wrote *Memoirs of a Geisha* after interviewing a number of geisha for background information about their world. The book was published in 1997, and spent two years on The New York Times bestseller list. Since then, it has sold more than four million copies in English and has been translated into thirty-two languages. In 2005, *Memoirs of a Geisha* was made into a prize-winning film, with Chinese actress Ziyi Zhang playing the central part of Nitta Sayuri.

Translator's Note

by Jakob Haarhuis, Professor of Japanese History,
New York University.

I first met Nitta Sayuri* in 1985, although she came to live in the United States in 1956. For the next forty years of her life she lived in elegant rooms, decorated in the Japanese style, on the thirty-second floor of New York City's Waldorf Towers.

If she had stayed in Japan, her life would have been too full for her to tell it in her memoirs. But here in New York she had time, and one day I asked if she would allow me to write her story.

"Well Jakob-san,"† Sayuri said to me. "I might tell my story if I can tell it to you."

This was because I knew Japan and I knew its history. Sayuri was clear that she wanted to *tell* me her story, not write it down. As a geisha, she would always talk to people, face-to-face; that was her life. She couldn't write a story in an empty room; she needed somebody with her, listening, talking to her. I suggested that she should talk into a tape-recorder, and she agreed.

But there were conditions. She wanted her story to be published only after her death and after the deaths of the men in her life. She did not want anybody to be embarrassed by her memoirs. That is also why she hides the identities of certain people behind names like "Pumpkin," although geisha use these names all the time in their work.

A geisha's work is to entertain men: geisha train for years to sing and dance and play instruments at parties. The men at these parties pay to have the geisha there. In Sayuri's time a really

---

* In Japanese the family name, *Nitta*, comes before the first name, *Sayuri*.
† In the polite Japanese way, Sayuri always called me *Jakob-san*—*san*, after the first name, is used like Mr., Mrs., or Ms.

1

popular geisha could earn one *ohana*—three Japanese yen—for every fifteen minutes that she spent at a party. That was enough to buy two bottles of wine in Kyoto in the 1930s.

The geisha, however, did not keep all the money herself. Some of it went to the teahouse where the party was held, some went to her dresser, some went to the *okiya*—the house where geisha live.

But the real money, at least for a top geisha, came from having a *danna*. No man could buy a top geisha for just one night. A man who wanted to be with a geisha for maybe six months or more could become her *danna*—if she was available and if he agreed fees with the mistress of her main teahouse. A *danna* paid a lot of a geisha's expenses. He paid for her make-up and maybe her lesson fees—because she never stopped learning to dance and to play instruments. And he still paid her fee (*ohana*) when she entertained him, but she went home with him afterwards.

Geisha usually don't talk about these things. Sayuri could only tell me about her life because she had left Japan and nobody in Japan had power over her any longer. So she talked into the tape-recorder and I listened.

Sometimes, still, I play her tapes during the evenings in my study and find it very difficult to believe she is no longer alive.

Chapter 1   The Little Fish Girl

I wasn't born and brought up to be a Kyoto geisha. I wasn't even born in Kyoto. I'm a fisherman's daughter from a little town called Yoroido on the Sea of Japan. We lived in a tiny house, high above the sea, and my father smelled like the sea even after he washed.

One day, many years ago, I was entertaining at a party in Kyoto and a man said he was in Yoroido only last week. I felt like a bird that has flown across the ocean and finds another bird that, knows its nest. I couldn't stop myself—I said:

"Yoroido! That's where I grew up."

The man didn't believe me.

"You can't mean it," he said, and laughed. "You, growing up in Yoroido! That's like making tea in a bucket."

Well, I'd never thought of Yoroido as a bucket, though it's not pretty. In those days, the early 1930s, it had only one road leading to the Japan Coastal Seafood Company, which sold all the fish that my father and the other fishermen caught.

My father was a very old man. I was twelve then, but from the day I was born I never looked like him at all. I always looked like my mother. We had the same strange eyes; you hardly ever saw eyes like ours in Japan. Instead of being dark brown like everyone else's, my mother's eyes were a shining gray and mine are just the same. It's the water in both our personalities. My father had wood in his personality; mother and I were full of water.

But all the water was running out of mother because of her illness. You could see every bone in her face getting harder and harder as the water dried out. Dr. Miura visited her every time he came to our village.

"Chiyo-chan," my father would say to me, "get the doctor a cup of tea."

My name back then was Chiyo. It was many years before I was known by my geisha name, Sayuri.

"Sakamoto-san," said the doctor to my father, one time, "you need to have a talk with one of the women in the village. Ask them to make a new dress for your wife. She shouldn't die in that old dress she's wearing."

"So she's going to die soon?" asked my father.

"A few more weeks, maybe," said Dr. Miura.

After that I couldn't hear their voices for a time. And then . . . "I thought I'd die first," my father was saying.

"You're an old man, Sakamoto-san. But you might have another year or two."

◆

One afternoon I came home from school and found Mr. Tanaka Ichiro walking up the path to my house. Mr. Tanaka's family owned the Japan Coastal Seafood Company. He didn't wear peasant clothes like the fishermen. He wore a man's kimono with kimono pants.

"Ah, Chiyo," said Mr. Tanaka. "Dr. Miura told me that your mother's sick. Give her this." He handed me a packet wrapped in rice paper, about the size of a fish head. "It's Chinese medicine," he told me. "Don't listen to Dr. Miura if he says it's worthless."

He turned to go but then turned back again. "I know a man," he said. "He's older now, but when he was a boy about your age, his father died. The following year his mother died. Sounds a bit like you, don't you think?"

Mr. Tanaka gave me a look that meant I had to agree with him. "Well, that man's name is Tanaka Ichiro," he continued. "I was taken in by the Tanaka family at the age of twelve. They gave me a new start."

The next day I came home from school and found Mr. Tanaka sitting across from my father at the little table in our house.

"So, Sakamoto, what do you think of my idea?"

"I don't know, sir," said my father. "I can't imagine Chiyo living anywhere else."

Part of me hoped desperately that Mr. Tanaka would adopt me, but I was also ashamed that I wanted to live anywhere except my little house above the sea. As Mr. Tanaka left, I heard my father crying.

◆

The next day Mr. Tanaka came to collect me in a little cart pulled by two horses. I thought we were going to his house but we drove to the train station. A tall, thin man met us there.

"This is Mr. Bekku," said Mr. Tanaka. And then he drove away again. Mr. Bekku gave me a look of disgust.

"Fish! Ugh! You smell of fish," he said.

When the train came, Mr. Bekku and I got on. As soon as we sat down he took out a comb and started pulling it through my hair. It hurt a lot and although I tried not to cry, in the end I did. Then he stopped doing it. The train went on and on, away from my home.

"Where are we going?" I asked, after a time.

"Kyoto," said Mr. Bekku. It was the only word he said to me on the long train journey. Kyoto sounded as foreign to me as Hong Kong or even New York, which I'd once heard Dr. Miura talk about.

I could see little of the city as we neared Kyoto station, but then I was astonished to see rooftop after rooftop, all touching, as far as the distant hills. I could never have imagined a city so huge.

Back in the 1930s there were still rickshaws in Kyoto. Mr. Bekku led me by the elbow and we climbed into a rickshaw. "Gion," Mr. Bekku said to the rickshaw driver. It was the first time I ever heard the name of the famous geisha area of Kyoto.

I fell back in the seat as the rickshaw driver picked up the poles and ran through the streets.

"Won't you please tell me where I'm going?" I said to Mr. Bekku.

For a moment I thought he wasn't going to reply. Then he said, "To your new home."

Soon we turned onto a street that seemed as broad as the whole village of Yoroido. I could hardly see the other side because of all the people, bicycles, cars, and trucks. I'd never seen a car or a truck before—except in photographs.

5

After a long time the rickshaw turned down an alley of wooden houses. We stopped and Mr. Bekku told me to get out. There in the doorway stood the most beautiful woman I'd ever seen, wearing a kimono more perfect than anything I'd ever imagined. It was water blue with white lines that curled like the current in a stream when she moved. It was pure silk. And her clothing wasn't the only extraordinary thing about her; her face was painted a kind of rich white, like a cloud lit by the sun.

This was Hatsumomo. I didn't know it then but she was one of the most famous geisha in Gion. She was a tiny woman; even with her black, shiny hair up high she came only to Mr. Bekku's shoulder.

"Mr. Bekku," said Hatsumomo. "What is that strong smell of fish? Could you take the garbage out later, please. I want to pass by."

There was no garbage there; she was talking about me.

Mr. Bekku led me past Hatsumomo into the small, elegant house. It was built up on stones, with enough space under it for a cat to crawl under. Inside, the hall had a wooden floor that shone in the yellow light of electric lamps.

A door slid back and a woman came out, smoking a pipe.

"This is the new girl, Mrs. Nitta," said Mr. Bekku.

"Ah, yes. The little fish girl," said the woman. "Come closer, I want to have a look at you. Heavens! What amazing eyes! You're a beautiful girl, aren't you?"

She spoke with the same peculiar accent as Mr. Bekku and Hatsumomo. It sounded so different from the Japanese spoken in my village that I had a hard time understanding her. I couldn't look at her, so I kept my eyes down on the wooden floor.

"There's no need to worry, little girl. No one's going to cook you. My name is Mrs. Nitta and this is the Nitta *okiya*."

I raised my eyes a little. Her kimono was yellow, with smooth, brown branches carrying lovely green and orange leaves. It was made of the most beautiful, delicate, thin silk. Then I raised my eyes higher and almost cried out in shock. The colors of her face were all wrong. Her eyelids were red like meat and her gums and tongue were gray. I later learned that this was due to a problem with her diet, but at the time I just stared in horror.

"What are you looking at?" said Mrs. Nitta, as smoke from her pipe rose from her face.

"I'm very sorry, ma'am. I was looking at your kimono," I told her. "I don't think I've ever seen anything like it."

This must have been the right answer—if there was a right answer—because she laughed, though the laugh sounded like a cough.

"So you like it, do you," she said, continuing to cough or laugh, I didn't know which. "Do you have any idea what it cost?"

"No, ma'am."

"More than you did, that's certain."

A young girl came out into the hall, carrying a wooden bucket full of water. She was a little older than me, thirteen or fourteen. Her body was thin, but her face was round. Even when she was a geisha in Gion many years later, everybody called her Pumpkin.

"Ah, Pumpkin," said Mrs. Nitta. "Get the little fish girl clean and get her out of those peasant clothes."

"Yes, ma'am," said Pumpkin.

She led me through the hall to a courtyard in the back. The bucket was heavy for her and when she put it down half the water spilled out over the dirt floor.

"Where on earth did you come from?" she said.

I didn't want to say I'd come from Yoroido. Pumpkin's accent was as strange to me as everybody else's. I was sure she wouldn't know where Yoroido was. I said instead that I'd just arrived.

"I thought I'd never see another girl my age," she said to me. "Why are your eyes that color?"

7

I didn't answer that, but took my clothes off so Pumpkin could wash me with a cloth she took out of the bucket. After that, she went to a room in the courtyard and got me a kimono. It was made of rough cotton in a simple dark blue pattern, but it was certainly more elegant than anything I'd worn before.

"I don't even want to know your name yet," said Pumpkin. "I have to learn new names all the time. Mrs. Nitta didn't like the last girl who came and she was only here a month."

"What will happen if they don't want to keep me?"

"It's better for you if they keep you."

"Why? What . . . what is this place?"

"It's an *okiya*. It's where geisha live. Our geisha is called Hatsumomo and we look after her and do everything for her. She earns all the money for the *okiya*. If you work very hard, you'll grow up to be a geisha yourself. But it takes years of training."

I had a sudden image in my mind of my poor, sick mother in bed, pushing herself up on one elbow and looking around to see where I'd gone. Tears came into my eyes before I could think how to stop them.

Chapter 2   No Escape

During those first few weeks in that strange place, I couldn't have felt worse if I'd lost my arms and legs, rather than my family and my home. I was confused and miserable, and I had no doubt that life would never again be the same.

But, strangely, during all that time, I felt an unreasonable warmth for Mrs. Nitta—something like the feeling that a fish might have for the fisherman who pulls the hook from its lip. Probably this was because I saw her no more than a few minutes each day while cleaning her room. She was always there, sitting at the table with an account book open in front her. The accounts were always organized, but nothing else was. She was messier even than Hatsumomo.

Hatsumomo lived like a queen in the *okiya* because she earned the income from which we all lived. And honestly, I've never seen a more astonishing-looking woman. Men in the street sometimes stopped and took their cigarettes from their mouths to stare at her.

Her room was the largest in the *okiya*, larger than my entire house in Yoroido. At first, I didn't understand why it was so much bigger even than Mrs. Nitta's. Then Pumpkin told me that in the past there'd been three or four geisha in the *okiya* and they'd all slept together in that one room, but Hatsumomo was the only geisha in the *okiya* now.

I always tried to clean the room as soon as Hatsumomo left for her dance lessons. I was worried about what might happen if she came back and found me alone in there. I hardly saw her because of the busy life she led, but I was still terrified of her.

One day, when I'd been in the *okiya* about a month, Mrs. Nitta led me upstairs to Hatsumomo's room, to watch her put on her make-up.

Before we went in, Mrs. Nitta warned me not to get in Hatsumomo's way. This is because, without her make-up, a geisha is like any other woman. She only becomes a geisha when she sits in front of her mirror to put her make-up on. And I don't just mean that this is when she begins to look like a geisha; this is when she begins to think like one too.

Hatsumomo told me to sit to the side of her and just behind. From there, I could see her face in the tiny mirror on her make-up table. She had half a dozen make-up brushes of different sizes and shapes. She told me what they were all called and how to use them.

"Now, why do you suppose I've shown you these things?" she said.

"So I'll understand how you put on your make-up," I said.

"Heavens, no! I've shown them to you so you'll see there isn't any magic to it. How sad for you! Because it means that make-up alone won't be enough to change the little fish girl into something beautiful."

Hatsumomo turned back to the mirror and sang quietly to herself. She painted her face and neck with a pale yellow cream, but left her eyes bare as well as the area around her lips and nose. Then she used the smaller brushes on these areas. I knew that in an hour or two, men would be looking with astonishment at that face; and I would still be here, cleaning the courtyard and the toilets in the *okiya*, washing the rice bowls, and sweating.

"I know what you're thinking," said Hatsumomo. "You're thinking you'll never be so beautiful. Well, it's perfectly true."

Then she sent me down to the room in the courtyard to get her a kimono. Outside the room I saw Mr. Bekku. I knew now that collecting young girls from fishing villages was not Mr. Bekku's only job. He was Hatsumomo's dresser and he helped her with the complicated job of dressing in the many elegant kimonos that the *okiya* owned.

"Oh, it's you," said Hatsumomo, when I returned with a kimono. "I thought I heard a little mouse or something. Tell me, are you the one who re-arranges all my make-up jars?"

"I'm very sorry, ma'am," I said. "I only move them to dust underneath."

"But if you touch them," she said, "they'll start to smell like you. And then the men will say to me, 'Hatsumomo-san, you smell just like a stupid girl from a fishing village.' I'm sure you understand that, don't you? But repeat it, just to be sure. Why don't I want you to touch my make-up?"

It was difficult to make myself say it, but in the end I did.

"Because it will start to smell like me," I said.

"That's very good. And what will the men say?"

"They'll say, 'Hatsumomo-san, you smell just like a stupid girl from a fishing village.'"

"Hmmm . . . there's something about the way you said it that I don't like."

Hatsumomo smiled and stood very close to me. I thought she was going to whisper in my ear, but she hit me across the face with her open hand.

I must have run out of the room because the next thing I can remember is Mrs. Nitta opening her door while she was still talking on the phone. I went into her room. Mrs. Nitta said, "Sorry," into the mouthpiece of the phone and added, "Hatsumomo is hitting the maids again."

When she was finished on the telephone, she called for Hatsumomo. "Hatsumomo! What have you done to Chiyo?"

Hatsumomo looked innocent. "She moved all my make-up jars, Mother, and she put her fingers in them."

I said nothing. Mrs. Nitta made me say "sorry" to Hatsumomo, and then she made me say it again in a correct Kyoto accent.

When Hatsumomo left, smiling, Mrs. Nitta said, "I don't think you understand your job here in the *okiya*." She nodded at the accounts. "We all think of only one thing—how we can help Hatsumomo be successful as a geisha. I don't want to hear that you've upset Hatsumomo again. If Pumpkin can stay out of her way, so can you."

"Yes, Mrs. Nitta."

But I couldn't keep out of Hatsumomo's way. She often hit me across the face when we were alone together. And she always criticized the way I looked, especially my eyes.

"I once saw a dead man fished out of the river," she said to me one time, "and his tongue was just the same color as your eyes."

Another time a man came to the *okiya* at night. He was wearing a traditional workman's jacket.

11

"You're a pretty one," he said to me in a low voice. "What's your name?"

I thought he must be a workman, though I didn't know what he was doing in the *okiya* so late. I was frightened of answering him, but I said my name.

Then Hatsumomo appeared. As the man went off toward her room, she stopped and spoke to me. She sounded like an angry cat.

"I haven't tried to make your life really miserable yet," she said. "But if you ever mention that a man came here to see me, that will change."

I wanted to say that she had succeeded in making my life really miserable, even if she hadn't tried. But I didn't say anything; I didn't want her to hit me across the face again.

About a week later, very late at night, I was coming back from taking a drink of water at the well in the courtyard. I heard the outside door open and Hatsumomo came in with another, tall, geisha. Hatsumomo was carrying a package and I could see that she and the tall geisha had been drinking. Hatsumomo drank a lot of beer and *amakuchi*, a kind of light, sweet wine.

Hatsumomo caught me in the hall. "This is our stupid maid," she said to the tall geisha. "She has a name, I think, but why don't you just call her 'The Little Fish Girl.'"

"Get us some more to drink, Little Fish Girl," said the tall geisha.

"Oh, be quiet, Korin," said Hatsumomo. "You don't need more to drink. Just look at this."

Hatsumomo opened the package. It was a beautiful kimono in different shades of green, with a pattern of red leaves.

Hatsumomo said, "Korin-san, guess whose kimono this is!"

"I wish it belonged to me," said Korin.

"Well, it doesn't," said Hatsumomo. "It belongs to the geisha we hate more than anyone else in the world."

Korin's eyes widened. "Mameha! You have one of Mameha's kimonos! How did you get it?"

"Her maid put the package down for a minute at the Kaburenjo Theater. Mameha is dancing there," said Hatsumomo. "Now, Little Fish Girl, go up to my room and get some ink and one of those brushes I use for writing."

I didn't understand why Hatsumomo wanted these things in the hall in the middle of the night, but of course I did what she said and brought them. Hatsumomo put the end of the brush in the ink. Then she put it into my hand and held my hand over the lovely kimono.

"Practice your writing, little Chiyo," she said.

"I can't do it, Hatsumomo-san," I cried. I heard the noise of a door opening upstairs, but I couldn't see anyone.

"What a shame, Little Fish Girl," said Hatsumomo, "because I definitely remember Mother saying that if you annoy me again you can't start your training as a geisha."

When the brush first touched the kimono, Korin wasn't happy with my first few uncertain brushstrokes. So Hatsumomo instructed me exactly how to ruin the beautiful kimono with ink. When I'd done it, she wrapped the kimono again.

Hatsumomo and Korin opened the door to the street and Hatsumomo told me to follow them. We walked up the alley to a street running along the Shirakawa Stream. Back in those days, the streets and alleys of Gion still had beautiful stone sidewalks. We walked along in the moonlight, past cherry trees whose branches dropped down into the black water. We went over a wooden bridge into a part of Gion I'd never seen before.

Hatsumomo and Korin stopped in front of a wooden door.

"You're going to give this kimono to the maid," Hatsumomo said to me. "Or if Miss Perfect herself answers the door, you may give it to her."

Even with so much fear in my heart, I couldn't help noticing how beautiful Hatsumomo was, next to the tall, long-faced Korin. I took the package with the ruined kimono and knocked at the door.

The maid who opened it wasn't a lot older than me. Behind her I saw a geisha and understood at once why they called her "Miss Perfect." Her face was a perfect oval.

"Asami-san!" said the perfect geisha. "Who's there?"

I put the package into the maid's hands and ran back to the *okiya* without waiting for Hatsumomo and Korin.

The next morning I saw the maid, Asami, again. She was coming out of Mrs. Nitta's room. Mrs. Nitta immediately sent me to bring Hatsumomo. Hatsumomo had seen Mameha's maid too, and she started speaking before Mrs. Nitta even opened her mouth.

"Oh, Mother, I know just what you're going to say. I felt terrible about the kimono. I tried to stop Chiyo before she put ink on it but it was too late. She must have thought it was mine. I don't know why she's hated me so much from the moment she came here..."

"Everybody knows that you hate Mameha," Mrs. Nitta replied. "You hate anyone more successful than you. Now you listen to me, Hatsumomo. I won't have this sort of behavior in the *okiya*, even from you. I have great respect for Mameha. And someone has to pay for the kimono. I don't know what happened last night but it's clear whose hand was holding the brush. Pumpkin saw the whole thing from her doorway. Chiyo will pay."

Later that day, in our tiny room upstairs, Pumpkin and I lay on our futons and she explained it all to me.

"I'm sorry," she said. "I tried to help you with Mrs. Nitta. But Hatsumomo's little trick with the kimono is going to cost you more money than you've ever imagined in your life."

"But... how will I pay?"

"When you begin working as a geisha, you'll pay the *okiya*

back for it. You'll also pay back everything else you'll owe—your meals and lessons; your doctor's fees, if you get sick. Why do you think Mrs. Nitta spends all that time in her room with her account books? You owe the *okiya* even for the money it cost to bring you here."

I thought of my father and Mr. Tanaka. In the weeks I'd spent in Gion, I'd certainly imagined that money had changed hands to bring me here. I saw my little house by the sea in my mind.

"I'm going home," I said to Pumpkin.

"Oh no!" said Pumpkin. "They'll bring you back. And then Mrs. Nitta will see you as a bad investment. She won't put money into someone who might run away again. She won't pay for your geisha lessons."

But I didn't care. At least, I didn't care then; I cared a lot later.

◆

Late that night I lay on my futon, waiting impatiently for darkness. If I could get home again, my mother wouldn't send me back. Maybe she didn't even know what father and Mr. Tanaka had done. I would look after her, she would get better . . .

I got up quietly and glanced at Pumpkin, sleeping next to me. I dressed in my peasant clothes and shoes and went out to the courtyard.

There was no moon. I went past the room where they keep the kimonos and pulled myself up to the low roof. Slowly, carefully, I felt my way along the roof on my hands and knees in the dark.

The roof of the building next door was a step lower than ours. I knew it was an *okiya*; all the houses in this block were. Someone would be waiting at the front door for the geisha to return and they would grab me by the arm as I dropped down. So I crossed to the next roof and then the next. And then one of my shoes came off.

I grabbed at it as it slipped down the roof and fell into the courtyard below. As I did this, I lost my balance and slid down the roof. I tried to stop myself sliding by holding onto the roof, but it was smooth and I fell, just as a woman came out into the courtyard. I hit the ground at her feet.

"What's this? It's raining little girls!"

I wanted to jump up and run away, but one whole side of my body hurt. I can't remember getting back to the Nitta *okiya* but I remember Mrs. Nitta calling the doctor. And I remember the terrible pain.

The next day Mrs. Nitta called me into her room. "I paid seventy-five yen for you," she said. "Then you ruined a kimono and now you've broken your arm so I have medical expenses too. Why should I pay for geisha training? You already owe more than you'll ever repay. Who would invest another yen in a girl who runs away?"

At that moment Hatsumomo came in.

"You're the most expensive maid in all of Gion," she said. "And you'll be a maid for the rest of your life." She smiled. "You'll never be a geisha now."

All that was in the fall. When spring came, the cherry trees were at their most beautiful in Marayama Park and along the Shirakawa Stream. A letter came addressed to me. It was from Mr. Tanaka and it informed me that my mother and my father were no longer on this earth.

Chapter 3   Hatsumomo and Mameha

For two years now, I'd lived the hard and boring life of a maid. My life stretched out before me like a long path going nowhere. Sometimes, out in the street, I watched girls of my age coming back from geisha school, talking to each other. Maybe they were just talking about what they were going to have for lunch, but to me their lives had a purpose. I, on the other hand, was going back to the *okiya* to wash the stones in the courtyard.

I walked down to Shijo Avenue and turned toward the Kamo River. The Minamiza Theater was showing a *kabuki* play that afternoon. It was *Shibaraku*, which is one of our most famous plays, though I knew nothing about *kabuki* theater at the time.

People streamed up the steps to the theater in the spring sunshine. Among the men in their dark western-style suits or kimonos, there were several geisha. They were so brightly colored that they were like bright fall leaves in the brown waters of a river.

The men and the geisha had a purpose—unlike me. I turned toward the Shirakawa, but even the water in that stream seemed to move with a purpose, running down toward the Kamo River and from there to Osaka Bay and the Inland Sea. Everything had a purpose except me. I threw myself onto the little stone wall at the edge of the stream and cried.

"Oh, the day's too pretty for such unhappiness," said a voice.

The man who had spoken had a broad, calm face. He was probably about forty-five years old, with gray hair combed straight back from his forehead. He was so elegant I couldn't look at him for long. I looked down.

There was a geisha with him. "Oh, she's only a maid!" said the geisha. "Really, Chairman, the *kabuki* play will be starting soon."

In those days I spent a lot of time in the streets of Gion, taking things to Hatsumomo at teahouses and bringing them back. On my journeys I'd often heard men called by titles like "Department Head" and "Chairman."

"Please, sir," I said to the Chairman. "Don't make yourself late because of me. I'm only a silly girl."

"Look at me a moment," he said.

I didn't dare disobey him. I looked up. He took a handkerchief from his pocket and wiped my tears. As he bent over me, I could smell the talcum powder on his smooth skin.

"Here you are, a beautiful girl with nothing to fear from life, and you're afraid to look at me. Someone's been cruel to you. Or maybe life has been cruel."

"I don't know, sir," I said, though of course I knew very well why I was crying.

"None of us find as much kindness in the world as we should," he told me. "Keep the handkerchief."

I knew then that I would always keep the handkerchief and I would never forget him. I closed my eyes for a moment and when I opened them he was gone.

I ran to Shijo Avenue and all the way to the eastern end of Gion, where the Gion Shrine stood. I climbed the steps to the shrine and began to pray. With my eyes shut tight and the Chairman's handkerchief pressed to my face, I prayed that somehow I could become a geisha.

♦

Pumpkin was still at geisha school. She was a slow learner. Every day she spent hours kneeling in the hall trying to learn to play her *shamisen*, one of the instruments that geisha play at parties. I walked past her because there was somebody at the door. We had a lot of visitors at the time. Mrs. Nitta's mother had just died, and people from all over Gion were coming to pay their respects. The visitor was the perfect geisha, Mameha.

I wasn't happy to see her because I wanted to forget the kimono incident, but then I remembered that Mameha hadn't actually seen me that night.

"What a beautiful girl," Mameha said to me. "What unusual gray eyes. What's your name?"

"Chiyo, ma'am."

The next day there was a maid among the visitors. After a

second or two I recognized Asami, Mameha's maid. To my surprise, Asami didn't go into the *okiya* to see Mrs. Nitta; she spoke to me at the door.

"Do you ever go out of the *okiya*, Chiyo?" she asked.

"Yes, often," I said. "Hatsumomo is always forgetting combs, or she wants a *shamisen*, and I bring these things to her at the teahouse. Or I go out and buy her food and beer."

"Good," said Asami. "Then meet me at the bridge over the Shirakawa Stream at three o'clock tomorrow."

I couldn't understand why she wanted me to do this, but it wasn't difficult to leave the *okiya*; Mrs. Nitta hardly noticed me. So of course I went to the bridge the next day. Asami led me to Mameha's apartment, the one I'd visited at night with Hatsumomo and Korin two years before.

"Chiyo is here, ma'am," the maid called out.

"All right, thank you, Asami," called Mameha from a back room.

Mameha's apartment wasn't large, but it was extremely elegant, with beautiful *tatami* mats on the floor that were obviously new and had silk around the edges, not the usual cotton.

At last Mameha came out from the back room, dressed in a lovely white kimono with a water design. I turned and bowed very low on the mats while she walked gracefully to the table. She arranged herself on her knees opposite me, drank delicately from the tea the maid served, and then said:

"Hatsumomo has driven other attractive girls out of Gion."

I felt strangely happy to hear that. I said, "I don't know what I did to make her hate me so much."

"Hatsumomo and I have known each other since I was a girl of six and she was nine," said Mameha. "She's no harder to understand than a cat. A cat that thinks another cat is eating from its dish . . ."

19

"But surely Hatsumomo doesn't see me as a rival, ma'am?"

"Not in the teahouses of Gion, maybe. But inside the *okiya*. You see, Mrs. Nitta never adopted Hatsumomo. If she had, Hatsumomo would be her daughter and Mrs. Nitta would keep all Hatsumomo's earnings. And Hatsumomo is a very successful geisha! Now, why would someone who's as interested in money as Mrs. Nitta not adopt Hatsumomo? There must be a very good reason, don't you think?"

This was all very new to me. I nodded and Mameha went on.

"Mrs. Nitta knows very well what sort of adopted daughter Hatsumomo would be. She would probably drive Mother out, or at least sell the *okiya's* collection of kimonos and retire. So Mrs. Nitta will never adopt her. But she might adopt you, Chiyo. She might adopt Pumpkin too, but I don't think Hatsumomo is worried about her."

"No. Pumpkin . . . She finds the geisha training difficult."

"I know. But you're not training at all, Chiyo. You can't become a geisha if you don't train."

I looked down and didn't say anything.

"You're a beautiful girl, Chiyo. And you don't look to me like someone who wants to live her life as a maid," said Mameha.

I said nothing. There was silence in the room for a moment. And then:

"You tried to run away, didn't you?"

With tears in my eyes, I told Mameha how I'd tried to escape along the rooftops.

"I'm sure you're an intelligent girl, Chiyo," said Mameha. "But I don't think that was a very intelligent thing to do. People like you and me, who have water in our personalities, don't choose where we'll flow to."

"Yes," I said. "I'm like a river that's stopped flowing because Hatsumomo is in the way."

"Yes, that's probably true," said Mameha, looking at me calmly.

"But rivers can wash away anything in their path—in time."

From the moment I arrived in Mameha's apartment, I wondered why she'd asked me to come. But now my eyes opened. Mameha and Hatsumomo obviously hated each other—that was clear from the kimono incident. But now Mameha knew there was a young girl at the *okiya* and saw a way of using me to get revenge on Hatsumomo. Maybe not just revenge; maybe she felt the time was right to be rid of Hatsumomo completely.

"Anyhow," Mameha went on, "nothing will change until Mrs. Nitta lets you start training."

"I don't have much hope of ever persuading her."

"Then I will," said Mameha.

Before I even had time to start feeling happy, Mameha was explaining her plan, beginning with the system of "Older Sister" and "Younger Sister," as it was in those days in Gion.

As I now know, there's a ceremony like a wedding when a geisha takes a young girl as her Younger Sister. Then the geisha introduces the Younger Sister to the owners of all the important teahouses, the ones that have the best parties.

The Older Sister takes her Younger Sister with her to entertain. Of course few men pay high *ohana* fees to sit and talk to a fifteen-year-old, so the Older Sister and the owner of the teahouse talk to a man until he does.

Eventually, the man who once needed so much persuading may become the Younger Sister's *danna*, when she's old enough to become a geisha herself.

Hatsumomo had in fact been an Older Sister, and a good one, to one or two younger geisha. But she wouldn't be a good Older Sister to me, I was sure of that. Instead of taking me to the Mizuki Teahouse and introducing me there, she would, I was sure, introduce me to the Kamo River. And then push me in.

♦

A few days after my visit to her apartment, Mameha went to see Mrs. Nitta. To my surprise, Mrs. Nitta sent for me.

"Now, Chiyo, you've been here in the *okiya* for a year . . ."

"Two years, ma'am."

"In that time I've taken hardly any notice of you. And then today, along comes a geisha like Mameha to say she wants to be your Older Sister! How on earth am I to understand this?"

Much later, when I knew more about Mameha, I could understand just how surprised Mrs. Nitta was. Mameha, as I later learned, was one of the two or three best-known geisha in Japan. Her Older Sister, Mametsuki, had the Prime Minister of Japan as her *danna*, before World War I.

But as I saw it then, Mameha was more interested in harming Hatsumomo than helping me. That's how Hatsumomo saw it too, when Mrs. Nitta sent for her. Mameha, of course, had asked for a fee to be my Older Sister but that didn't fool Hatsumomo.

"Really, Mother . . ." Hatsumomo said to Mrs. Nitta. "Mameha doesn't need Chiyo to make money. Do you think it's an accident that she's chosen a girl who lives in the same *okiya* as I do? Mameha would probably be Older Sister to your little dog if she thought it would drive me out of Gion."

"Really, Hatsumomo," said Mrs. Nitta. "Why would she want to drive you out of Gion?"

"Because I'm more beautiful. Does she need a better reason? She wants to humble me by telling everyone, 'Oh please meet my new Younger Sister. She lives in the same *okiya* as Hatsumomo, but they've given her to *me* for training instead.'"

"I can't imagine Mameha behaving that way," said Mrs. Nitta, quietly. "Hatsumomo, you, of course, will be Pumpkin's Older Sister," she added.

"Of course," said Hatsumomo. She spoke to Mameha for the first time, as Mameha looked calmly back at her. "If you think you can make Chiyo into a more successful geisha than Pumpkin, you can expect a big surprise."

Mameha ignored her. "Will you arrange for Chiyo to start geisha training at school?" she said to Mrs. Nitta.

"Of course," said Mrs. Nitta, bringing her account books. "I had no idea what a fine day this would be."

And it *was* a fine day for Mrs. Nitta. Two famous geisha were fighting each other to increase the income of her two young girls. She needed to adopt one of the girls, so that the *okiya* continued when she died. She would choose the one who earned the most; all that girl's earnings would go to the *okiya*.

Chapter 4   From Chiyo to Sayuri

Pumpkin had come to the Nitta *okiya* six months before I arrived. She was born in Sapporo. Her mother died when she was five and her father sent her to Kyoto to live with an uncle. Then the uncle lost his business and he sent Pumpkin to Mrs. Nitta.

Pumpkin was the kind of girl who could get fat quickly, if she had the chance. But they didn't give us much to eat at the *okiya*, just rice at most meals, with soup once a day and a little dried fish twice a month. Sometimes in the night I'd hear Pumpkin's stomach making noises from hunger.

On our first walk to geisha school together, she suddenly said, "Oh Chiyo-chan! Doesn't it make you hungry?"

We were passing a small Shinto shrine. Inside there were sweet-rice cakes on shelves, but Pumpkin didn't mean them. Outside the doorway, just on the edge of the street, there was a small piece of fish on the sidewalk. You could buy fish like that in the street; somebody had dropped the last piece. Two flies were walking around in circles on it.

"Pumpkin," I said, "if you're hungry, take a sweet-rice cake from that shelf. Don't eat the fish, the flies have got it."

"I'm bigger than they are," said Pumpkin, and she bent down and picked up the fish.

"Pumpkin!" I cried out. "Why don't you eat the sidewalk?"

"OK," she said, and she bent down and licked the sidewalk with her tongue.

When Pumpkin got to her feet again, she clearly couldn't believe what she'd done. But she put the dirty piece of fish in her mouth and chewed it all the way to the block where the school was.

I now know that only some of that block was the school itself. Part of it was actually the Kaburenjo Theater—where the geisha of Gion perform *Dances of the Old Capital* every spring.

I followed Pumpkin into a long wooden building next to the theater; this was the school. There was a smell of roasted tea leaves which even now makes my stomach turn over. Halfway down a hall was a big, traditional-style Japanese classroom. We put our names down for four classes that morning—*shamisen*, dance, tea ceremony, and a kind of singing we call *nagauta*.

Some people call a *shamisen* a Japanese guitar, but actually it's a lot smaller than a guitar. It has a thin wooden neck, and the entire instrument can be taken apart and put into a box or bag so you can carry it about.

Pumpkin tried to play *shamisen* before the class started, but even after more than two years, as I knew from listening to her practice, she wasn't very good at it. The room filled with girls who began practicing *shamisen*.

Then the teacher came in. She was a tiny old woman with a high voice. Her name was Teacher Mizumi and this is what we called her to her face. But her name, Mizumi, sounds like *nezumi*—mouse; so behind her back we called her Teacher Mouse.

Pumpkin led me to the front of the room, where we bowed to Teacher Mouse.

"May I introduce Chiyo to you, Teacher," Pumpkin said, "and ask you to teach her because she is a girl of very little talent."

Pumpkin wasn't being rude; this was just the way people spoke back then, when they wanted to be polite. My own mother would have said it the same way. Teacher Mouse looked at me and then said, "You're a smart girl. I can see it just from looking at you. Maybe you can help your sister with her lessons."

Of course she was talking about Pumpkin.

Then we went back to our places, and Teacher Mouse called a girl to the front of the room. After bowing to the teacher, the girl began to play. In a minute or two Teacher Mouse told her to stop and said all sorts of unpleasant things about her playing; then she shut her fan and waved it at the girl to send her to the back of the room.

This continued for more than an hour, then it was Pumpkin's turn. I could see she was nervous and she played badly, even for her. Nobody could tell what tune she was trying to play.

Teacher Mouse banged the table and told her to stop. She hit her fan on the table to give Pumpkin the tune. She put Pumpkin's fingers in the right place on the *shamisen*—but nothing helped. She sent Pumpkin away to the back of the class and Pumpkin walked slowly, with tears in her eyes.

I was pleased that Pumpkin's other classes weren't as painful to watch as the first one had been. In the dance class, for example, the students practiced the moves together, with the result that no one looked too bad. And Pumpkin wasn't the worst dancer in the group. The singing class, later in the morning, was more difficult for her because she couldn't hear a tune. But there again, the students practiced together, so Pumpkin was able to hide her mistakes by moving her mouth a lot and singing quietly.

After I'd been going to these lessons for some time, I started

25

learning to play a small drum we call a *tsutsumi*. At parties at teahouses, geisha sing with a *shamisen* only. But when they perform at the theater, for example in *Dances of the Old Capital* every spring, six or more *shamisen* players play together with drums and other instruments. Geisha learn to play all these instruments.

Most of the time, except for Teacher Mouse, the teachers played the tune first and then we all tried to play it back. And then the teacher would call out from the front things like, "The girl at the back, you must keep your finger down, not up in the air."

In all the lessons you were corrected if you spoke in anything except a Kyoto accent, or if you walked badly or sat or knelt badly.

The last lesson every morning was tea ceremony. Geisha are trained to prepare tea for guests in the traditional way and to pour the tea into beautiful cups. Even the guests must hold the cups in a special way, so it's a little like a dance, danced while kneeling.

All these skills needed practice, but of course in the afternoon I still had to clean the *okiya*, which Pumpkin didn't.

In the beginning Pumpkin and I practiced *shamisen* together every afternoon. We had great fun together; it was the time of day I looked forward to most.

Then one afternoon, while Pumpkin was teaching me a tune, Hatsumomo came into our room. We didn't even know she was in the *okiya*.

"Oh, look, it's Mameha's future Little Sister!" she said to me. "I thought *you* were stupid, Little Fish Girl, but Pumpkin here is even more stupid."

Poor Pumpkin put her *shamisen* down like a dog putting its tail between its legs. "Have I done something wrong?" she asked.

Hatsumomo pulled Pumpkin's lip so hard she screamed.

"Now I know," said Hatsumomo, still pulling the lip, "that they call you Pumpkin because your head really is full of pumpkin. Now put your *shamisen* away and go to my room."

Pumpkin started to take her *shamisen* apart; her lip was bleeding. Hatsumomo turned to me. "You'll have to find yourself another little friend," she said. "After Pumpkin and I have had our talk, she won't speak to you again. Will you, Pumpkin?"

Pumpkin nodded; she had no choice, but I could see how sorry she felt. We never practiced *shamisen* together again.

I told Mameha what had happened the next time I went to see her at her apartment.

"If Pumpkin isn't allowed to speak to you, then you mustn't speak to her either," said Mameha. "You'll only get her into trouble, and she'll have to tell Hatsumomo what you say. You may have trusted the poor girl in the past, but you mustn't any longer."

I felt so sad at this. I blew on my tea and started to drink.

"Really, Chiyo, you must stop blowing on your tea in that way," said Mameha. "You look like a peasant! Leave it on the table until it's cool enough to drink."

"I'm sorry," I said. "I didn't know I was doing it."

Mameha asked me to pour her a cup of tea. The pot was empty, but she asked me to do it anyway.

"No!" said Mameha, when I'd poured as elegantly as I could. "You have a lovely arm, and beautiful skin. You should make sure every man who sits near you sees it at least once. Why do you think the sleeves on kimonos are so big? It's so that men can see our arms when we pour tea. Now do it again."

I imagined myself inside a teahouse, sliding open the door of a *tatami* room. The men turned their heads to look at me, and I saw the Chairman there among them. I smelled his talcum powder. In his smooth fingers he held a teacup. I poured the tea for him, showing him my arm, and felt his eyes on me as I did it.

"That's better," said Mameha.

♦

27

Some people say that when a young girl has finished her training and she's ready to become a novice geisha, she's like a bird that's ready to leave the nest. I don't agree at all! A bird only has to grow big enough and then fly. I worked for two hard years at *shamisen*, singing, tea ceremony, and many other skills. I learned to speak in a Kyoto accent and not to behave like a peasant. But finally, one day, the time of the ceremony to make me a novice geisha was at last near.

The first step was to have my hair done the way all novice geisha wore it. Gion had quite a lot of hairdressers in those days; Mameha's worked in a room above a fish restaurant. I had to spend nearly two hours waiting for my turn and I'm sorry to say that the smell of dirty hair in there was terrible. The hairstyles that geisha wore in those days were so complicated and expensive that nobody went to the hairdresser more than once a week.

When my turn came at last, the hairdresser put me over a large sink in a position that made me think he wanted to cut my head off. Then he poured a bucket of warm water over my hair and began to wash it by rubbing soap hard into my head. I was almost in tears from the pain.

"Cry if you have to," said the hairdresser. "Why do you think I put you over a sink?"

He thought that was a joke, but I didn't think it was funny. I was in there for two hours, but my problems with my hair were just beginning. If a novice geisha goes to sleep on a pillow after she has had her hair done, it will spoil it and she will have to go back to the hairdresser again the next day.

So novices sleep on a special pillow called a *takamakura*. You don't put your hair or your head on this *takamakura*. You put your neck on it and then go to sleep without moving.

And then there's the kimono. In the beginning I could hardly walk at all in the special kimono that novices wore. I was worried that I might fall over. Young girls wear a very long *obi*—the wide belt around the kimono. It's longer than the *obi* that older women wear. The *obi* is very heavy and so long that it will go from one end of a room to the other. The kimono itself is also very heavy, with long sleeves.

And the colors on a novice's kimono ... Years later I met a famous scientist from Kyoto University. He'd been to Africa and seen all the brightly colored monkeys; the most colorful animals in the world. But he said that a novice geisha from Gion in kimono was brighter than any of them.

One sunny October afternoon I was wearing my novice's kimono and had my hair in novice style, when Mameha and I left Mameha's apartment and walked along the Shirakawa. We were watching the leaves of the cherry trees float down to the water. Many people were out walking there and all of them bowed to Mameha. In many cases they also bowed to me. I wondered if the Chairman would think I looked beautiful. I found myself looking out for him in the street, as I often did.

"After two years of training you're getting rather well-known, don't you think?" said Mameha. "People are always asking me about the girl with the lovely gray eyes. You won't be called Chiyo much longer."

"Does Mameha-san mean to say ... "

"You're going to make a fine geisha," said Mameha, "but you'll make an even better one if you think about what you are saying with your eyes."

"I didn't know I was saying anything with them," I said.

"A woman can say more with her eyes than with any other part of her body," said Mameha, "especially in your case. So I think we can say that you are ready to start as a geisha as soon as you can make a man faint with your eyes."

"Mameha-san!" I said. "If I could do that, I'm sure I would know about it by now."

But I wanted to be a geisha so much that I would have tried to make a tree faint if Mameha had told me to. The first man we saw was so old, though, that he looked like a kimono full of bones. He didn't notice me at all, so we turned into Shijo Avenue.

There was a delivery boy carrying some lunch boxes.

"Make him drop his boxes," said Mameha, and she crossed the street and disappeared.

I didn't think it was possible for a girl of sixteen to make a young man drop something just by looking at him; maybe these things happened in movies and books. But I noticed that the young man was already looking at me the way a hungry cat looks at a mouse. And I also noticed that although most of the streets in Gion didn't have a curb, this one did.

I looked up at him, smiled, then looked down again. After a few more steps I did the same thing again. When we were close, I moved into his path and looked him right in the eye. He tried to move out of my way, but his feet hit the curb and he went down. Well, I couldn't help laughing! And I'm happy to say the young man began to laugh too. I helped him pick up his boxes, gave him a little smile before he bowed to me more deeply than any man had ever bowed before, and then he went on his way.

♦

The ceremony took place at the Ichiriki Teahouse, which is certainly the best-known teahouse in all of Japan. You can't see most teahouses from the street, but the Ichiriki, on Shijo Avenue, is as obvious as a palace—which is what it looked like to me.

Two of Mameha's Younger Sisters and Mrs. Nitta came to the ceremony, which lasted about ten minutes. Mameha and I drank *sake* together. I drank three times and then passed her the cup and she drank three times. We did this with three different cups and then it finished.

From that moment, I was no longer known as Chiyo. I was the novice geisha Sayuri.

Chapter 5   The Novice Geisha

The 1930s was the time of the Depression,* so there were fewer formal parties for me to go to than Mameha would have liked. But we went to small parties and not only at the teahouses. We went to swimming parties on the river, we went to sightseeing parties and *kabuki* plays.

At some of the parties there were writers and *kabuki* actors. But I'm sorry to say that the usual geisha party was more boring. The party was often given by a small company for another small company they did business with. The conversation usually wasn't very intelligent. A man might turn to the geisha beside him and say, "The weather certainly is unusually warm, don't you think?" And the geisha would reply with something like, "Oh, yes, very warm."

After the conversation there would usually be a drinking game, or the geisha would try to get all the men singing. Sometimes the geisha played children's games with the businessmen, to keep them happy.

The formal parties were the worst. There was one at Kansai International Hotel. Guests sat shoulder to shoulder in a U-shape around the outside of a big room with *tatami* mats on the floor. The geisha had to move inside the U-shape, kneeling in front of each guest long enough to pour *sake* and chat. It wasn't exactly exciting, and it was even less exciting for a novice like me than for Mameha. Whenever Mameha introduced herself to a guest I did the same, bowing very low and saying, "My name is Sayuri; I'm a novice." After that I said nothing and no one said anything to me.

Because I was a novice, I was not supposed to drink *sake*— novices should seem childlike. But sometimes the men poured a

*The Depression: from 1929 to 1939 world economic activity—world trade—slowed and almost stopped. Millions of people all over the world had no job and very little money.

drink and made me drink it. On those occasions Mameha always rescued me, saying, "It's your first day in Gion, Sayuri. You can't get drunk. Just wet your lips." And I would "drink" the *sake* with my lips closed.

It was just after one of these occasions—I remember the man who wanted me to drink *sake* had very bad skin—that Hatsumomo and Pumpkin first started following us. We were at the Komoriya Teahouse. I'd just dried my lips from the *sake* when I saw Hatsumomo smiling at me from the other side of the table. Mameha saw the fear in my face and we left.

That victory for Hatsumomo was quickly followed by many others. We went to a party at Kyoto University. Hatsumomo and Pumpkin appeared ten minutes after we'd arrived.

"Really, I don't think there's anything more difficult than being a novice," Hatsumomo said to the man who was talking to me. "Don't you think so, Sayuri?"

Hatsumomo had two reasons for making this "innocent" remark. First, the man I was talking to forgot all about me and had eyes only for Hatsumomo. Secondly, it was meant to remind us that Pumpkin was no longer a novice. She'd moved to the next stage in becoming a geisha apprentice; she was going to a lot of parties, and she was earning a lot more in *ohana* fees than me.

I couldn't think of a smart reply to Hatsumomo, but luckily Mameha spoke for me:

"You're certainly right about the novice time being a difficult time of life for you, Hatsumomo-san. Though, of course, you were more awkward than most."

Hatsumomo just smiled. Men don't come to parties to listen to geisha arguing, so, again, we left the party.

Mameha began to take me to parties that she thought Hatsumomo wouldn't know about, but Hatsumomo and Pumpkin always appeared just a few minutes after we arrived.

I knew that Mameha was also worried that Hatsumomo was telling stories, lies, about me. It seems that she'd driven rivals out of Gion before by doing this.

Things were bad but they soon got worse. Mameha and I had just made ourselves look rude by leaving a party shortly after we arrived, to get away from Hatsumomo and Pumpkin, when Mameha pulled me into an empty room and held me by the wrist.

"Did you tell that terrible woman where we would be tonight?" she asked.

"No, Mameha-san. I didn't know myself where we were going until I got to your apartment."

"Yes . . . Yes, of course. Then how does she . . .? Is it my maid? But no Asami wouldn't . . . Come on!"

"Where are we going?"

"Naga Teruomi just arrived in town from Tokyo. Do you know him? He's one of Tokyo's best young musicians. Anyway, he's giving a very small party this evening. We'll be safe there; hardly anybody knows he's even in Kyoto."

The party was at a very small teahouse near the Gion shrine, in east Gion. Ten minutes after we arrived, Hatsumomo and Pumpkin came in. Hatsumomo quickly got everybody's attention and continued her conversation from the last party.

"I was just saying how difficult it is to be a novice," Hatsumomo told the entire party; everybody was listening to her. "I'll tell you a story about a novice . . . Oh no, I can't—there's one here, at this party."

This, of course, was me.

"I want to hear this story," said one of the men, just as Hatsumomo knew he would.

"Oh very well. But I'll tell it to you only if you all promise that you won't think of this poor girl here as you listen. Picture some other girl in your mind."

Hatsumomo really was a devil. The men might not have

pictured the story happening to me earlier, but they certainly would now.

"Let me see, where was I?" Hatsumomo began. "Oh yes. Well, this novice I mentioned . . . I can't remember her name, but I ought to give her one or you will confuse her with this girl here. Tell me, little novice . . . what's your name?"

"Sayuri, ma'am," I said, my face hot with nervousness. Everybody at the party looked at me and then looked back to Hatsumomo.

"Sayuri! How lovely! Somehow it doesn't suit you. Well, let's call this novice in the story 'Mayuri.' Oh yes, I remember now, Mayuri had funny-colored eyes. Some people thought they were the color of dead worms."

I glanced at Mameha, but I could see there was nothing she could do. Hatsumomo, smiling, continued:

"Anyway, this novice became an apprentice and then a geisha very quickly, and one day it was time for her *mizuage*."

Some of the men at the party, drunk on *sake*, laughed at this. A geisha's *mizuage* was taken the first time she spent a night with a man. Some men paid a high fee to be the first with a geisha.

Hatsumomo looked lovelier than ever as she continued her devilish story: "Well, after the *mizuage*, and this is the first time this has ever happened in Gion, the man who had thought himself so lucky at first, asked for his money back. Do you know why?"

There was a roar of laughter. Of course the drunken men had several suggestions, some ruder than others. Some of them glanced at me as they spoke.

Hatsumomo was laughing too. "No, really, this is serious. It seems that her whole body . . . " And here Hatsumomo waved her delicate hands to show the line of my body. "Her whole body . . . was the body of an old woman. Her face was still sixteen or seventeen but underneath, below the neck, well her . . . "

34

Hatsumomo was now looking at me directly as she began to describe my body as that of an old woman. Mameha led me from the room, without stopping to say good-bye to Naga Teruomi.

Mameha and I went down the steps of the teahouse. On the bottom step she stopped and waited. At last a young maid came to see us out—the same maid who had shown us up the stairs earlier.

"What a difficult life you must have as a maid!" Mameha said to her. "Probably you want so many things and have so little money to spend. Tell me, what will you do with the money you have just earned?"

"I haven't earned any money, ma'am," she said, but I could see she was lying.

"How much money did Hatsumomo promise you?"

The maid looked at the floor. It wasn't until this moment that I understood what Mameha was thinking. As we learned some time afterward, Hatsumomo had paid at least one maid in every first-class teahouse in Gion to telephone the Nitta *okiya* as soon as they saw Mameha and me.

Out in the street Mameha said, "I'm trying to think where we can go, but . . . I can't think of a single place. If that woman has found us here, she can find us anywhere in Gion. I think you should go back to your *okiya*, Sayuri, and stay there until I can think of a plan."

I ought to have been attending formal parties every night, and ten or fifteen informal parties too, but instead I stayed in the *okiya* practicing *shamisen* and dance. My income from party fees was now zero.

In the next few days I went to Mameha's apartment several times, each time hoping that she had thought of a plan, but she hadn't.

"I'm sorry, but you must stay in the *okiya* for a little longer," she said. "I'm more determined than ever to destroy that evil woman, but until I've thought of a plan it will do you no good at all to follow me around Gion."

Of course I was disappointed to hear it, but Mameha was quite right. Another evening like Naga Teruomi's party would do me more harm than good as a geisha.

Happily, Mameha could still take me with her to entertain outside Gion, where Hatsumomo couldn't pay maids to tell her where we were. I went to Kobe when Mameha opened a new factory. Another time I went with Mameha and the president of the Nippon Telephone Company on a tour of Kyoto in a luxury car. This was the first time I saw how poor some people were in the Depression. We drove along the river, south of the city, and I saw dirty women feeding their babies under the trees and men with no shoes and no hope drinking next to them. I realized that even with Hatsumomo and her cruelty to me, I had a relatively fortunate life during the Depression.

♦

One day Mameha and I were walking across Shijo Avenue Bridge when it was clear to me from her face that something was wrong.

"What is it Mameha-san?" I asked.

"Well, I'll tell you because you'll only hear it from someone else," she said. "Your little friend Pumpkin has won the apprentice's prize this year. She earned more money from *ohana* than any other apprentice geisha in Gion."

"But . . . but how?" I said.

Mameha sighed. "In Gion," she began, "a very popular geisha can always make sure her Younger Sister earns more than anyone else if she doesn't mind damaging her own reputation."

Mameha explained that apprentices like Pumpkin were expected to attend about five parties an evening and build relationships. Instead of this, Hatsumomo was taking Pumpkin with her everywhere, to as many as twenty parties a night. The men were paying two lots of *ohana* charges for a geisha and an apprentice who were spending very little time at the party. In the end both Hatsumomo's and Pumpkin's reputations would suffer. But before that Hatsumomo would have got what she wanted.

"Hatsumomo wants Pumpkin to look good so Mrs. Nitta will adopt her," Mameha finished up. "If Pumpkin is made daughter of the *okiya*, Hatsumomo is safe. As Pumpkin's Older Sister, Mrs. Nitta won't throw her out. Do you understand what I'm saying, Sayuri? If Pumpkin is adopted, you'll never be free of Hatsumomo, and it's possible that you'll be the one they throw out."

A few days after our conversation, Pumpkin told me that Mrs. Nitta was going to adopt her. It was definite.

Chapter 6   Nobu Toshikazu

"We still have a few weeks before Mrs. Nitta adopts Pumpkin," said Mameha. "We are going to have to take action, and quickly."

I nodded unhappily, not knowing what action we could take; but it seemed that at last Mameha had a plan.

"Do you know about *mizuage*?" Mameha asked me.

The question reminded me of Hatsumomo's terrible story, so I looked down and said nothing.

Mameha looked at me kindly. "The word *mizu* means 'water' and *age* means 'raise up.'"

Mameha then told me what happens when a man spends the night with a woman. She said that some men would pay a lot to be the first one to spend the night with a geisha—the *mizuage* night. Mameha planned to introduce me to two men who she hoped would bid against each other for my *mizuage*.

"And then one of them would become my *danna*?" I asked. I can't say I felt very enthusiastic about that. When I thought about things like that, I always thought about the Chairman. I thought about him all the time anyway.

"Not necessarily," said Mameha. "For some men the *mizuage* is enough. Other men will be a geisha's *danna* only after her *mizuage*."

"So the Baron . . . " I said, but then I stopped because of the look on Mameha's face.

Baron Matsunaga Tsuneyoshi was Mameha's *danna*. He paid for Mameha's lovely apartment, where we were having this conversation. Before World War II there were quite a few barons in Japan but Matsunaga Tsuneyoshi was one of the richest of them. He lived in Tokyo, where his family controlled one of Japan's large banks, but he owned a lot of land around Kyoto. He visited Mameha whenever he was in the area and he was the *danna* of another geisha in Tokyo too.

"No, the Baron didn't take my *mizuage*," Mameha said, in a way that made it clear that the subject was closed.

"It's strange that Hatsumomo hasn't got a *danna*," I said, to change the subject.

Mameha smiled, pleased to change the subject and pleased with my growing skill at conversation, which of course is an important skill for a geisha.

"She had a *danna* at one time," said Mameha. "And of course she has a lot of admirers. But somehow she angered the mistress of the Mizuki, her main teahouse, so the mistress always told men that Hatsumomo wasn't available. The men probably thought that she already had a *danna*."

Then I remembered the evening years ago when a man visited the *okiya* late at night and spent the night with Hatsumomo. In the morning, Pumpkin and I heard Hatsumomo crying because the man said he was going back to his wife and didn't want to visit her anymore. Pumpkin said he was a cook at one of the restaurants in Gion. She also told me that if Mrs. Nitta ever found out that Hatsumomo brought men back to the *okiya*, the situation would be serious, even for a geisha as great as Hatsumomo.

"What are you thinking about Sayuri?" asked Mameha.

"Nothing, Mameha-san," I replied.

Mameha smiled. "You are growing up, Sayuri," she said.

♦

Mameha was still attending a morning engagement when I arrived at her apartment. Her maid showed me into the dressing room to help me with my make-up, and afterward brought in the kimono that Mameha had chosen for me. Mameha had let me wear her kimonos before, but in fact it's unusual for a geisha to lend her kimonos to a Younger Sister. Mameha was showing great kindness to me.

I didn't realize it at the time, but the beautiful kimono that was laid out on the futon for me was well-known in Gion; people who saw it probably thought of Mameha at once. When she allowed me to wear it, she was transferring some of her magic as a geisha to me.

It was the loveliest kimono I'd ever worn—orange silk with a silver waterfall pouring from the knee into a deep blue ocean. The *obi* was brown with gold in it. When Mr. Itchoda, Mameha's dresser, had tied the *obi*, I put the Chairman's handkerchief in it. I'd brought it from the *okiya*. I always put it in the sleeve when I wore a kimono. Then I looked at myself in the mirror and my mouth fell open in amazement at how I looked.

It was amazing to me that Mameha had arranged for me to look so beautiful; but then when she returned to her apartment, she herself changed into a fairly plain kimono. She had the quiet beauty of a pearl, as she always did, but when we walked down the street together, the women who bowed at Mameha were looking at me.

From the Gion Shrine, we rode north in a rickshaw for half an hour, into an area of Kyoto I'd never seen. Along the way Mameha told me we'd be attending a *sumo* wrestling exhibition as the guests of Iwamura Ken, who had started Iwamura Electric in Osaka. Iwamura's right-hand man, Nobu Toshikazu, President of Iwamura Electric, would also be there. Nobu was quite a fan of *sumo*. He was also one of the men Mameha hoped would bid for my *mizuage*.

"I should tell you," Mameha said, "that Nobu looks a little . . . strange. If you behave well, you will impress him greatly."

Mameha gave me a look: she would be disappointed in me if I didn't. But at least we wouldn't have to worry about Hatsumomo, Mameha told me, maybe to change the subject. Tickets to the exhibition had been sold out weeks before.

At last we climbed out of the rickshaw at the campus of Kyoto University. Mameha led me up a small path, with western-style buildings on both sides of us. The windows were made into tiny glass squares by sticks of painted wood. I hadn't noticed how much Gion seemed like home to me, until I noticed myself feeling out of place at the University.

Smooth-skinned young men stopped to watch as Mameha and I walked past, and then they talked and joked with each other about us. To them we were creatures from another world.

The Exhibition Hall was huge, filled with the noise of the people and with smoke from roasted sweet-rice cakes. In the center was a square where the wrestlers would try to push each other out of the wrestling area to win the contest.

Our places were on *tatami* mats in the front. Our hosts were there and I saw a man waving his hand to Mameha; I knew at once that he was Nobu. Even from a distance the skin of his face looked like a melted candle. At some time in his life he must have suffered terrible burns. Much later I found out that when he was a young soldier in the Japanese army, he had been injured in the bombing outside Seoul in 1910, at the time when Japan took Korea. He had been in pain ever since.

Next to Nobu, kneeling on the same *tatami* mat at the front, wearing a man's striped kimono, was the Chairman. The Chairman was looking at me with apparent curiosity. The blood came rushing into my face, making my feet go cold.

"Chairman Iwamura . . . President Nobu," Mameha said, "this is my new Younger Sister, the apprentice Sayuri."

By now I was an apprentice, like Pumpkin. And even a sixteen-year-old apprentice had heard of Iwamura Ken. But I never imagined for a moment that Iwamura Ken was the man I'd met by the Shirakawa Stream. This was the man I still dreamed about every night; the man whose handkerchief was in my *obi* at that very moment.

I picked up a small teapot and held the sleeve of my kimono out of the way to pour. To my astonishment and joy, the Chairman's eyes moved to my arm. And then suddenly Mameha stopped talking. For a moment I didn't realize what the problem was. And then I noticed the teapot again. In my happiness that the Chairman was watching me, I hadn't noticed that it was empty. It had been empty even when I'd picked it up.

Mameha laughed. "You can see what a determined girl she is, Chairman," she said. "If there had been a single drop of tea in that pot, Sayuri would have poured it out."

"That certainly is a beautiful kimono your Younger Sister is wearing, Mameha," the Chairman said. "Do I remember seeing it on you, back during your days as an apprentice?"

"It's possible, I suppose," Mameha replied. "But the Chairman has seen me in so many different kimonos over the years, I can't imagine he remembers them all."

A long look passed between the Chairman and Mameha. Then the Chairman said, "Well, I'm no different from any other man. I never forget beauty. But I can never remember which *sumo* wrestler is which. They all look the same to me."

Mameha leaned across in front of the Chairman and whispered to me, "What the Chairman is really saying is that he doesn't like *sumo*."

"Now, Mameha," said the Chairman, "if you're trying to get me in trouble with Nobu . . . "

"Chairman, Nobu-san has known for years how you feel!"

The Chairman smiled and then spoke to me. "Sayuri, is this your first time at *sumo*?"

I'd been waiting for some excuse to speak with him, but before I'd even taken a breath to answer, several wrestlers came into the Exhibition Hall. Our heads turned and the audience went silent. Nobu had his head turned away from me. I couldn't keep my eyes off the terrible burns on the side of his face and neck and at his ear, half of which was not there at all. Then I saw that the sleeve of his jacket was empty. I hadn't noticed that earlier. Nobu had only one arm.

I turned back to the Chairman. As an apprentice geisha I was free to sit as quietly as an arrangement of flowers if I wanted to, but I was determined not to let this opportunity pass.

"The Chairman asked if this is my first time at *sumo*," I said. "It is, and I would be grateful if the Chairman could explain it to me."

"If you want to know what's happening," said Nobu, "you'd better talk to me. What's your name, apprentice? I didn't hear what Mameha said."

I turned away from the Chairman with as much difficulty as a hungry child turns away from a plate of food.

"My name is Sayuri, sir," I said.

"Sayuri is a very pretty name—though pretty names and pretty girls don't always go together."

I wondered if his next remark was going to be, "What an ugly Younger Sister you've taken on, Mameha," or something like that, but to my relief he said, "Here's a case where the name and the girl go together. You have especially beautiful eyes. Turn toward me, Sayuri, so I can have another look at them."

I looked at him, as well as I could; then I was rescued by two wrestlers going into the square.

"The first wrestler who is pushed out of that square is the loser," said Nobu. "It might look easy, but how would you like to push a huge man like that out of a square?"

"I suppose I could come up behind him and shout, so he jumped out," I suggested.

This was a mistake. "Be serious," Nobu said.

I know it wasn't a very smart thing to say, but this was my first attempt at joking with a man. Then the Chairman leaned toward me.

"Nobu-san doesn't joke about *sumo*," he said, quietly.

"I don't joke about the three things that matter most in life," Nobu said. "*Sumo*, business and war."

The announcer said the winning wrestler's prize would be a great deal of money given by Nobu Toshikazu. Nobu was annoyed and said to the Chairman, "The money isn't from me. It's from Iwamura Electric. I'm sorry, Chairman. The man is a fool."

"There's no mistake, Nobu. After everything you have done for me and the company, it's a small thing to do."

"The Chairman is too kind," said Nobu. "I am very grateful."

Later I found a magazine article about the Chairman's company. I discovered that Iwamura Electric nearly went bankrupt in the early 1920s. Nobu found some new investors and saved the company. "I owe Nobu everything," said the Chairman, in the article. He said that Nobu was more like a brother than a business partner.

The announcer welcomed us all and said the wrestlers were *yokozuna*—that's the highest rank in wrestling. "Just like Mameha's position in Gion," as Nobu explained to me. But if Mameha spent as long getting ready before she did anything as these two elephants did, she would never get another party invitation. The wrestlers spent five minutes throwing salt all over the square and staring at each other, then one pushed the other out and it was finished.

The audience clapped and shouted, but Nobu said, "That wasn't very good."

Two more wrestlers went into the square. I felt that one ear was connected to my mind and the other to my heart. On one side I listened to what Nobu told me—and much of it was interesting. But I was always listening to the Chairman's voice on the other side, as he talked with Mameha. I loved the sound of him.

The last fight was between a star wrestler called Miyagiyama, who was not quite as enormous as the others, and an especially huge man called Saiho.

"*Hataki-komi*," said Nobu, excitedly. "Miyagiyama will use *hataki-komi*, you wait and see."

And he did. The larger Saiho rushed at Miyagiyama and the smaller man used *hataki-komi*, which means he used the energy of the bigger man's attack against him. He moved out of the way when Saiho ran at him and brought his hand down on the man's neck as he ran past, so the rush of Saiho's own attack took him out of the square.

Later, on our way back to Gion, Mameha turned to me excitedly in the rickshaw.

"We're going to use *hataki-komi* against Hatsumomo," she laughed. "She thinks her rush around the teahouses has earned more money for Pumpkin than I have for you, but we will see her running out of Gion like Saiho ran out of the square. Just keep Nobu-san interested in you. Everything depends on him and one other man. One of them will be your rescuer."

I felt sick inside at the thought of this. I wanted my rescuer to be the Chairman.

44

Chapter 7   Dr. Crab

Two weeks passed, and then one day I received a note to come to Mameha's apartment the following afternoon. By now I was used to beautiful kimonos waiting for me on the futon, so I wasn't surprised at the lovely medium-weight bright red and yellow silk kimono, which showed leaves in a field of golden grass. But I was surprised to find a tear in the back of it, large enough to put two fingers through.

"Asami-san," I said to Mameha's maid, "the most upsetting thing . . . this kimono is ruined."

Of course I'd told Mameha long ago about the part Hatsumomo made me play when her kimono was ruined with ink, all those years ago. But I certainly didn't want her to think I'd ruined another kimono.

"No, Miss," said Asami. "Mameha-san borrowed it from an *okiya* down the street. She knows it's torn. The underskirt is torn in the same place."

I'd already put the underskirt on. I reached down and felt my thigh through the hole. Asami was right.

"Mameha-san was very clear that she wanted you to put it on," added Asami.

This made very little sense to me, but I did as Asami said. When at last Mameha rushed in, I asked her about it while she re-did her make-up.

"I told you that my plan is to have two men bidding for your *mizuage*," said Mameha. "You met Nobu two weeks ago. The other man has been out of town until now, but with the help of this torn kimono, you're going to meet him now."

The mention of Nobu's name made me depressed again because a man will never have a relationship with a geisha if a close friend has been with her for the night. Meeting the

45

Chairman seemed only to have put him further away from me. Mameha's next words made me even more depressed.

"Sayuri, we're just going to put a little cut in your skin. Just a little one, so you can go to the hospital and meet a certain doctor. You know the man I mentioned to you? He's a doctor."

"Can't I just say I have a stomach ache?"

I meant this seriously, but Mameha and Asami couldn't stop laughing.

"Sayuri, we only need to make you bleed just a little, just enough so the Doctor will be willing to look at you," smiled Mameha.

Asami brought a knife from the kitchen and I lay on the futon with a cloth under me and my eyes closed. I bit my lip as soon as I felt the tip of the knife. A little river of blood ran down my leg.

"Good girl," said Mameha. "When you are asked how you cut your leg, this is your answer. You were trying to go to the bathroom in your kimono, and you fell onto something sharp. You don't know what it was because you fainted. Make up all the details you want; just be sure that you sound very childish. And act helpless at the hospital. Let me see you do it."

I lay my head back on the futon and let my eyes roll up. Mameha wasn't at all pleased.

"I didn't say act dead. I said act helpless."

I practiced on the way to the hospital, while Mameha pulled at my kimono to make sure I still looked attractive. At the hospital Mameha gave me one final instruction.

"Remember, Sayuri, we want the Doctor to see you looking as innocent and as helpless as possible. Lie back and look weak."

My leg hurt, so I had no difficulty at all with this. A nurse showed us down a long hall to a dusty room with a wooden table. A moment later the door opened and in came Dr. Crab.

Of course, his name wasn't really Dr. Crab, but the reason for the name was obvious enough. He walked bent forward with his elbows out, in a way that made him look just like a crab.

He was obviously a very thorough man. He spent a couple of minutes closing the door, making sure he'd done a good job and that it wouldn't open again. After this he took a small case from his pocket and carefully took out a pair of glasses. He looked at me and gave a little nod and finally he looked at Mameha. He was pleased to see Mameha; his mustache moved a little.

"I'm so sorry to trouble you, Doctor," said Mameha. "But Sayuri has such a bright future and now she has cut her leg. I thought you were the only person to help her."

"Exactly," said Dr. Crab. "Now, could I have a look at the cut?"

"I'm afraid Sayuri gets weak at the sight of blood, Doctor," said Mameha. "It might be best if she turned away and let you look at the cut. It's on the back of her thigh."

"I understand perfectly. Could you please ask her to lie on her stomach on the examining table?"

I couldn't understand why Dr. Crab didn't ask me himself, but to seem obedient I waited until I'd heard the words from Mameha. Then the doctor lifted my kimono as high as he could and put some smelly liquid on the cut with a cloth.

"Sayuri-san," said Dr. Crab, "please tell me how you cut yourself."

I began to tell Dr. Crab the story I'd agreed with Mameha. Finally, Dr. Crab finished with the smelly liquid and told me how to look after the cut for the next few days. Then he put my kimono down again and put away his glasses.

"I'm sorry you have ruined such a fine kimono," he said. "But I'm certainly happy at the chance to have met you. Mameha-san knows I'm always interested in new faces."

"I'm very pleased to have met you too," I said.

"I may see you one evening quite soon at the Shirae

Teahouse," he said. "Let me see. I'll be there . . . " Then he put his glasses back on again so he could look at a little book he took out of his pocket. "Yes, I'll be there two evenings from now. I do hope to see you."

Mameha assured him we'd be there. In the rickshaw on our way back to Gion she told me I'd done very well.

♦

Later that week I was invited to the Ichiriki Teahouse by Iwamura Electric and then I was invited again without Mameha. Mameha told me not to stay too long, so it would look like I had plenty of other parties to go to. So, after an hour I bowed and said good-bye, as though I were on my way to another party. For some reason, Hatsumomo didn't appear.

Then Iwamura Electric gave a party that was the smallest party I'd attended in Gion, with only two other geisha and four men, including the Chairman and Nobu. This time, Hatsumomo appeared. Her lovely smile grew as soon as Nobu entered the room.

Hatsumomo had missed my first meeting with Nobu at the wrestling, as there had been no maid there to let her know we were there. But she knew all about my "romantic relationship," as she called it, with Nobu, who she called The Fried Man. This was a cruel reference to his face.

So I decided to show her the romantic relationship she'd come to see. I began by touching my neck and my hair all the time, as if I was worried about the way I looked. Then I leaned toward Nobu. I touched the flowers I wore in my hair until they fell into his lap. The flowers fell onto the *tatami* mat between his crossed legs. I'd planned to get the flowers out from his lap, with girlish laughter, but I didn't have the confidence to do it.

Nobu picked the flowers up himself and turned them in his hand, instead of giving them back. "Get the young maid who greeted me," he said to me. "Tell her I want the package I brought."

I did as Nobu asked and returned to the room. Everyone was waiting and watching me. Nobu was still holding my flowers and didn't take the package from me. "I was going to give it to you later, on your way out," he said to me. "But I think I should give it to you now."

He nodded toward the package in a way that suggested I should open it. I felt very embarrassed, but I opened the package and found a fabulous gold comb to be worn in the hair, in the shape of a half-circle.

"It's an antique I found a few days ago," Nobu said.

The Chairman moved his lips but seemed to have trouble speaking. Eventually he said, "Well, Nobu-san! I have never known you do such a thing before." His face was pale and he looked shocked.

Hatsumomo stood and walked toward me. She knelt near me, took the gold comb and put it in my hair as gently as a mother with a baby.

"Isn't she the loveliest creature," she said to Nobu, nodding at me. Then she gave a deep sigh and soon afterward she left the party.

I was still an apprentice at that time, not a geisha, but for the first time in my life I felt like a geisha. Hatsumomo had not found a way to hurt me at the party; I'd beaten her, using my geisha skills. Of course, Hatsumomo still made trouble for me at parties when she could, and sometimes she won and I lost. But my *ohana* fees began to increase; I was in demand at parties, and I was becoming well-known.

◆

When an apprentice geisha becomes available for *mizuage*, she gives boxes of *ekubo* to the men she knows. These *ekubo* are sweet-rice cakes and most geisha give them to at least a dozen men, maybe more. But I would give them only to Nobu and the Doctor—if we were lucky.

Dr. Crab hadn't appeared at the Shirae Teahouse, as we'd arranged with him at the hospital. I managed to find Pumpkin alone, when she went out to buy *sake* for Hatsumomo, and on a bench by the Shirakawa Stream I finally managed to persuade her to tell me what had happened.

"Pumpkin, please listen to me," I said. "I wouldn't ask this of you if there was any other way. But I don't want to go back to being a maid and that is what will happen if Hatsumomo has her way. Either that or I will have to leave the *okiya*. Pumpkin, please."

Suddenly tears ran down Pumpkin's big cheeks, as if they'd been waiting to fall for years.

"Oh, I'm so unhappy, Chiyo-chan," she said. She still called me Chiyo and I still called her Pumpkin, like everybody else did.

"Pumpkin, just tell me, how did Hatsumomo stop Dr. Crab coming to the Shirae Teahouse?"

"Oh that," said Pumpkin. "That was easy. The maid at the teahouse told us you and Mameha were on the guest list for a party there. Hatsumomo knew at once. Very few important people go to the Shirae. Crab only goes there because he knows it from his student days, before he made all his money. Hatsumomo thought of him at once. And besides, he is known in Gion as a '*mizuage* specialist.' As soon as Hatsumomo thought of him, she knew what Mameha was planning."

"But why didn't he come?"

"Well, you know Hatsumomo. She can make anyone believe anything. She told the Doctor that you have a boyfriend who spends the night with you in the *okiya*. Hatsumomo described him; he's a cook in a restaurant around the corner. She said she

50

knows about it but Mrs. Nitta doesn't and Mrs. Nitta would throw you out of the *okiya* if she ever found out."

I could just imagine how much Hatsumomo must have enjoyed her little story, telling Dr. Crab that her own lover had come to see me. I asked Pumpkin if there was anything more, but she said no.

I thanked her many times for helping me, and told her how sorry I was that she'd had to spend these last few years as a slave to Hatsumomo.

Pumpkin put her head on my shoulder and cried.

♦

Mameha went around all the teahouses in Gion, asking people to tell her if Dr. Crab appeared. After a few nights, word came that he was at a teahouse named the Yashino. I rushed to Mameha's apartment to change into a kimono and then we left for the Yashino with a box of *ekubo*.

The Yashino was a new teahouse, built in the western style. Instead of *tatami* mats on the floor, the room we were shown into had armchairs and a sofa. I didn't feel comfortable in the chairs but Mameha told me not to kneel on the floor. She sounded angry. Then she went off to find Dr. Crab.

Dr. Crab didn't look at all happy when Mameha brought him into the room. "I prefer to get back to my party," he said when he saw me. "Please excuse me."

"Sayuri has brought something for you, Doctor," Mameha told him. "Just for a moment, if you please."

After that I think Mameha forgot about using the chairs because when Dr. Crab sat down, we both knelt down in front of him.

"Please accept these *ekubo*, Doctor," I said, offering him the rice cakes.

"Why are you giving me these?"

"I'm so sorry, Doctor," said Mameha. "I told Sayuri that you would enjoy receiving *ekubo* from her. I hope I'm not mistaken?"

"You are mistaken. Maybe you don't know this girl as well as you think. I have an excellent opinion of you, Mameha, but I think less of you for introducing this girl to me. I suggest you ask her about the boy who works at a restaurant near her *okiya*."

I was pleased he'd mentioned this himself; Mameha and I had feared he might not.

"So that's the problem!" Mameha said to him. "You must have talked with Hatsumomo. She has been spreading this story all over Gion. It's completely untrue."

"Why would Hatsumomo do that?"

"Ever since Sayuri was given an important part in *Dances of the Old Capital*, Hatsumomo has been telling these stories. It seems she wanted the part for her own Younger Sister, a rather large girl called Pumpkin."

The doctor looked at me for the first time. I did my best to look like a star dancer who has had lies told about her.

"I don't like to say this, Doctor," Mameha continued, "but Hatsumomo is a known liar. You can't believe anything she says."

"It's the first I've heard of it."

"Well," said Mameha, "either I'm lying to you now or Hatsumomo was lying to you before. You have to decide which of us you know better, Doctor."

When the Doctor left, walking his crab-like walk, he took the *ekubo* with him.

One afternoon, a few days later, Mameha came to the *okiya* and took me into Mrs. Nitta's room to tell me that bidding for my *mizuage* had begun.

Chapter 8   Sayuri Becomes a Geisha

Before my *mizuage* night, I had to "turn the collar"—change from an apprentice to a geisha. The change is called "turning the collar" because an apprentice wears a red collar on the underskirt which shows below her kimono, while a geisha wears a white one. I turned seventeen around the same time, in the summer of 1938.

The day I turned my collar was one of the happiest of Mrs. Nitta's life; or at least she acted more pleased than I've ever seen her. I didn't understand it at the time, but it's perfectly clear to me now what she was thinking. A geisha, unlike an apprentice, is available to a man for more than just pouring his tea, for the right fee. And because of my connection with Mameha and my increasing popularity in Gion, that fee was probably going to be large.

In the end, Dr. Crab offered more than Nobu for my *mizuage*, 11,500 yen. Until that time, this was the highest amount ever paid for a *mizuage* in Gion, and possibly in any of the geisha districts of Japan. My *mizuage* fee was more than a worker earned in a year. Even Mameha's *mizuage*, although a few years earlier, cost only 8,000 yen.

The *mizuage* fee was, of course, the reason Mrs. Nitta adopted me. If she hadn't adopted me, some of that money would have fallen into my hands—and I can just imagine how my new Mother would have felt about that!

But, as Mother said to me, "One day the *okiya* will be yours." We were in her room, sitting at her table, with smoke from her pipe filling the room. I couldn't think of anything to say, but she didn't seem to notice. "You and I will perform a ceremony next week," she said. "After that, you'll be my daughter just as if you'd been born to me."

I was finding it difficult to concentrate on what she was saying; the changes were so great. Mother was telling me that as daughter of the *okiya* I would sooner or later move into the big room used by Hatsumomo. Hatsumomo would have to share with Pumpkin.

I watched Mother's gray mouth moving and slowly realized that this had always been Mameha's plan but I'd never really believed it would happen.

As this thought came into my mind, the door opened and Hatsumomo herself was there.

"What do you want?" Mother said. "I'm busy."

"Get out," Hatsumomo said to me. "I want to talk with Mother."

"If you want to talk with me," Mother said, "you may ask Sayuri if she'll be kind enough to leave."

"Be kind enough to leave, Sayuri," said Hatsumomo in a funny voice that was supposed to sound like me.

And then, for the first time in my life, I spoke back to her without the fear that she would punish me for it.

"I'll leave if Mother wants me to," I told her.

"Mother, would you be kind enough to make The Little Fish Girl leave the room?" Hatsumomo said.

"Don't talk about Sayuri like that," said Mother. "Now, what do you want?"

The tiny figure of Hatsumomo stood over us, so near that I could smell her perfume.

"Poor Pumpkin's just come running to me, very upset," she began. "I promised her I'd speak with you. She told me something very strange. She said, 'Oh, Hatsumomo! Mother's changed her mind!' But I told her I doubted it was true."

"I don't know what she meant. I certainly haven't changed my mind about anything recently," said Mother.

"So you haven't changed your mind about adopting her?"

"What gave you that idea? I was never going to adopt Pumpkin."

It hurt me to hear Mother say this, not only because it wasn't true, but for Pumpkin's sake. Hatsumomo looked at me with hatred.

"You haven't helped Pumpkin in her apprenticeship as well as I'd hoped," Mother said to Hatsumomo. "She was doing well for a time, but lately . . ."

"You promised, Mother," said Hatsumomo. It was frightening to hear her. She didn't sound like a person at all, more like an animal—a wounded cat.

"Sayuri will be my daughter in one week," said Mother. "Between now and then you must learn to treat her with respect. When you go downstairs, ask the maid to bring tea for Sayuri and me."

♦

It's strange, and very hard to explain, but the world looked different to me after *mizuage*. Pumpkin, who hadn't yet had hers, now seemed inexperienced and childlike to me, even though she was older than me. Mother and Hatsumomo and Mameha had all done it, of course, and I was probably much more aware than they were of having had a shared experience.

After *mizuage* a geisha wears her hair in a new style, with a red silk hairband not a patterned one. For a time, I was so aware of which geisha had red silk hairbands and which had patterned ones that I hardly seemed to notice anything else while walking along the street. I had a new respect for the ones who had been through *mizuage*, and felt more experienced than the ones who hadn't.

But I didn't just see the world differently after *mizuage*. My day-to-day life changed as well because of Mother's new view of me. Mother was the sort of person who puts a price on everything. Before my *mizuage*, I don't think it made any difference to her that Hatsumomo was making trouble for me in

Gion when she could. But now I had a high price on me, so she stopped Hatsumomo's troublemaking.

I didn't ask her to do it, and I don't know how she did it. Probably she just said, "Hatsumomo, if your behavior causes trouble for Sayuri and costs this *okiya* money, you'll be the one to pay it."

Inside the *okiya*, life was almost pleasurable. As the adopted daughter I ate when I wanted. I chose my kimono first instead of waiting for Pumpkin to choose hers.

Of course, I didn't mind that Hatsumomo hated me because I was treated better, but when Pumpkin passed me in the *okiya* with a worried look, avoiding my eyes, that caused me real pain.

♦

With my *mizuage* behind me, Dr. Crab disappeared from my life almost completely. I say "almost" because I still saw him at parties in Gion; but he was a true "*mizuage* specialist" and so had no more interest in me.

At the next Iwamura Electric party I sat myself next to the Chairman, not Nobu. I didn't mean to, but I ignored Nobu. The Chairman was friendly when I poured his *sake*, but he didn't really look at me. But I noticed that Nobu was staring at me angrily because I wasn't talking to him. So before the evening was over I spent a bit of time with him and I was careful never to ignore him again after this.

A month or two passed, and then one evening during a party, I mentioned to Nobu that Mameha had arranged for me to appear at a festival in Hiroshima. I wasn't sure he was listening when I told him, but the next day when I returned to the *okiya* after my lessons, I found in my room a new travel case he'd sent me as a gift.

I felt terribly ashamed of myself for thinking I could simply forget Nobu after he was no longer needed to bid for my *mizuage*. I wrote him a note of thanks for the travel case and told him I looked forward to seeing him at the next big party that Iwamura Electric planned in two months' time.

But something strange happened. Just before the party, I received a message saying I wasn't needed after all. I thought maybe they had canceled the party. But I was at the Ichiriki anyway, for another party, and I met a geisha called Katsue, who had just been to the Iwamura party.

"It's a good party," she said. "There must be twenty-five geisha there and nearly fifty men . . ."

"And . . . Chairman Iwamura and Nobu-san are both there?" I asked her.

"Not Nobu," said Katsue. "Someone said he went home sick this morning. But the Chairman is there; why do you ask?"

I can't remember what I said to that. But I felt deeply worried. I'd always somehow imagined that the Chairman wanted my company as much as Nobu did. Now I wasn't so sure; maybe Nobu was the only one who cared about me.

♦

The next day, Mother asked to see me in her room.

"This time next month you'll have a *danna*," she said.

"A *danna*? But, Mother, I'm only eighteen . . ."

"Yes. Hatsumomo didn't have a *danna* until she was twenty. And of course that didn't last . . . You should be very pleased."

"Oh, I am very pleased," I said untruthfully. "But . . . having a *danna* will take a lot of my time and . . . I'll earn less from party fees."

This didn't deceive Mother. "Leave the business decisions to me," she said. "Only a fool would turn down an offer like the one Nobu Toshikazu has made."

My heart nearly stopped when I heard this. I suppose it was obvious that Nobu would one day propose himself as my *danna*.

He'd made an offer for my *mizuage* and since then he'd asked for my company at parties more than any other man.

But reaching the Chairman was the one hope that had helped me through my training. I couldn't give myself to the one man who would put him out of reach forever. I almost ran across Gion to see Mameha.

Mameha knew all about it. "Nobu-san is a good man," she said, "and very fond of you. I understand you may find Nobu difficult to look at, but . . ."

"Mameha-san, it isn't that. Nobu-san is a good man, as you say. But, Mameha-san . . . I don't know how to say it . . . this is never what I imagined!"

"What do you mean? Nobu-san has always treated you kindly."

"But Mameha-san, I don't want kindness!"

"Don't you? I thought we all wanted kindness. Maybe what you mean is that you want something more than kindness. And that is something you're in no position to ask for."

Chapter 9   General Tottori

Mother gave Mameha a cautious glance because she didn't know why Mameha was there, but then she gave a little bow and thanked her for coming. I didn't know why Mameha had come either. We all sat at the table, looking at each other over Mother's account books.

"I'm sure you must be very pleased," Mameha began, "that Sayuri will soon be taking a *danna*. And at only eighteen years of age! How young to be taking such a big step."

"Mameha would have done well to take a *danna* at that age herself," Mother replied. "My advice to you, Mameha-san, is that you do what you are good at, like teaching Sayuri that pretty way of rolling her eyes. You may leave the business decisions to me."

"I would never discuss business with you, Mrs. Nitta. I'm sure you know more about these things . . . But may I ask? Is it true the most generous offer has come from Nobu Toshikazu?"

"His has been the only offer. I suppose that makes it the most generous."

"The only offer? What a pity . . . The results are so much better when several men compete. Don't you agree?"

"A hundred yen is a hundred yen," said Mother, "whether it comes from this man or that one."

"I'm sure that's true," said Mameha, softly. "Still, it's disappointing. Because another man has expressed interest in Sayuri, General Tottori Junnosuke . . ."

At this point I stopped listening to the conversation because I understood for the first time that Mameha was trying to rescue me from Nobu. I certainly hadn't expected that. I had no idea why she had changed her mind since our last conversation. Maybe she had her own reasons that were nothing to do with me. My mind was full of these thoughts, until I felt Mother's hand on my arm.

"Well?" she said.

"Ma'am?"

"I asked if you know the General."

"I've met him a few times, Mother," I said. "He comes to Gion often."

I don't know myself why I said that. The truth is I'd met the General more than a few times. He came to parties in Gion every week. He was a bit short, smaller than I am, in fact. But he was one of those men who everybody looked at all the time. He moved around a lot, always smoking cigarettes, so he seemed to live in a cloud of smoke.

The last time I saw him he was slightly drunk and talked to me for the longest time about all the ranks in the army. Everybody was talking about the army around this time because what we now call World War II, against America and England, had just started.

General Tottori found it very funny when I confused all the army ranks. His own rank was *sho-jo*, which means "little general"—the lowest of the generals.

But now Mameha was telling Mother that the General had a new job. As Mameha explained it, the new job was like a housewife going to market. If the army needed ink, for example, the General's job was to make sure it got ink at the best possible price.

"With his new job," Mameha said, "the General can now become a *danna*. And he can be a big help to the *okiya*."

"No!" said Mother. "The army men never take care of a geisha the way the businessmen or the barons do. They never offer a reliable income."

"Mrs. Nitta, until now in this war, we have been lucky in Gion," Mameha said. "But the shortages will affect us if the fighting continues."

"I'm sure they would affect us," Mother said. "But this war will end in six months."

"And when it does, the army will be even more important. Mrs. Nitta, don't forget that General Tottori can get you anything you want for this *okiya*, whether the war ends or not."

We all discovered later that Mameha was right. Her argument certainly had a big effect on Mother. She glanced at the teapot and you could almost see her thinking, "Well, I haven't had any trouble getting tea; not yet . . . though the price *has* gone up . . ." And then, without even realizing what she was doing, she put one hand inside her *obi* and squeezed her silk bag of tobacco.

◆

During September of that year, General Tottori and I drank *sake* together at a ceremony at the Ichiriki Teahouse. This was the same ceremony I'd first performed with Mameha when she became my Older Sister, and later with Dr. Crab just before my *mizuage*.

In the weeks afterward, everybody congratulated Mother on finding me such a powerful *danna*. Everybody except Nobu, who told me briefly and angrily at a party that General Tottori wasn't good enough for me, and then walked away.

On that very first night after the ceremony, I went on the General's instructions to a small hotel with only three rooms in the northwest of Kyoto, called the Suruya Inn. By this time I was used to luxury and that decaying inn was a shock. The walls were wet and the *tatami* mats were so full of water that they made a noise when I stepped on them. When General Tottori came, he turned on the radio and sat drinking a beer.

As the months passed, my twice-weekly meetings with the General at the Suruya Inn became nothing more than an unpleasant routine. Sometimes I wondered what it might be like with the Chairman; and to tell the truth I was a little afraid that I might not like it, just as with the Doctor and the General.

♦

During the summer of 1939 I was busy with parties, meetings with the General, and dance performances. In the morning when I tried to get up from my futon, I often felt like a bucket filled with nails. I wondered how much I was earning through all my efforts, but I never really expected to find out. So I was very surprised when Mother called me into her room one afternoon and told me I'd earned more in the past six months than both Hatsumomo and Pumpkin combined.

"That means," she said, "that the time has come for you to exchange rooms with them."

If you'd asked me, while I was still a young woman, to tell you the turning point in my relationship with Hatsumomo, I would

61

have said it was my *mizuage*. But even though it's true that my *mizuage* made me safe from Hatsumomo, the real turning point occurred the day we exchanged rooms.

To explain this, let me tell you something that Admiral Yamamoto Isoroku once said during an evening at the Ichiriki Teahouse. I can't pretend I knew the Admiral well—he's usually described as the father of the Japanese Navy—but I went to the same parties on a number of occasions. Parties usually grew louder after the Admiral arrived.

At one party the Admiral had, as usual, just won a drinking game. Someone made a joke about him always winning, but the Admiral didn't laugh. He said he never had any doubts about winning.

One of the geisha said, "Oh come on! Everybody loses sometimes, Admiral, even you!"

"I suppose it's true that everyone loses occasionally," said the Admiral. "But never me."

Some people at the party thought this was arrogant, but I didn't. Someone asked him the secret of his success.

"I never try to defeat the man I'm fighting," explained the Admiral. "I try to make him less confident. When you are more confident than your opponent, you will win."

The day I moved into Hatsumomo's room, I became more confident than her.

Tigers walk alone, and everyone knows that a wounded tiger is the most dangerous of the big cats. For that reason Mameha insisted that we follow Hatsumomo around Gion for the few weeks after we exchanged rooms.

So every evening, except when she had an engagement she couldn't miss, Mameha came to our *okiya* when it got dark and we followed Hatsumomo. On the first night we did this, Hatsumomo pretended to find it amusing. By the end of the fourth night she was looking like a hunted animal. On the fifth night she turned to us and raised her hand to hit Mameha. I screamed, which must have made Hatsumomo stop and think about what she was doing. She stared at us for a moment with eyes burning, before all the fire suddenly went out of her and she walked off.

Plenty of people saw what had happened and a few came over to see if Mameha was all right. She said she was fine and then said, sadly, "Poor Hatsumomo! It must be just as the doctor said. She really does seem to be losing her mind."

There was no doctor, of course, but Mameha's words had the effect she'd hoped for. Soon a rumor spread all over Gion that a doctor had said Hatsumomo was losing her mind.

For years Hatsumomo had been very close to the famous *kabuki* actor Bando Shojiro VI. Shojiro was an *onna-gata*, which means that he always played women in the theater. Once, in a magazine interview, he said that Hatsumomo was the most beautiful woman he'd ever seen. He said that on the stage, he tried to be as much like her as possible to make himself seem attractive. Not surprisingly, whenever Shojiro was in town, Hatsumomo visited him.

One afternoon I learned that Shojiro would attend a party later that evening at a teahouse in the geisha district of Pontocho, on the other side of the river from Gion.

Around nine o'clock Mameha and I arrived at Shojiro's party. It was outdoors; the teahouse had built a big wooden platform above the water. It was beautifully lit with paper lamps, and the river was gold with the lights of the restaurants on the opposite bank. Shojiro was in the middle of telling a story in his high voice, as we arrived. Hatsumomo looked frightened at the sight of us.

Mameha knelt right next to Hatsumomo, which I thought was very brave of her. I sat further away. Someone immediately asked Mameha to play the *shamisen* and dance, which she did.

63

Shojiro seemed fascinated. After her performance Shojiro, who was a dancer himself, asked her to sit next to him. He turned his back on Hatsumomo.

Nobody knows better than Mameha how to keep a man's attention, and soon Shojiro was charmed into acting some of his best-known performances just for Mameha. Then he started imitating other actors. One of these imitations, of an actor called Bajuri who had performed *kabuki* in London to great praise, ended with Shojiro holding Mameha and kissing her all over her face. Even Mameha looked surprised. Everyone else on the platform clapped and cheered. Everyone except Hatsumomo.

"You are making a fool of yourself," Hatsumomo told Shojiro.

"Oh, Hatsumomo-san," said Shojiro, "you're jealous!"

"Of course she is!" said Mameha. "Now you must show us how the two of you make friends again. Go on, Shojiro-san. Don't be shy! You must give her the same kisses you gave me!"

Shojiro pulled Hatsumomo to her feet. Hatsumomo didn't want to stand, but Shojiro did it in the end. He bent to kiss her, then pulled his head back, screaming. Hatsumomo had bitten him on the lip.

"Hatsumomo-san, please," said Mameha, as if she was speaking to a child. "As a favor to me . . . *do* try to calm down."

I don't know if it was the effect of Mameha's words, or whether maybe Hatsumomo really was losing her mind, but she threw herself at Shojiro, kicking and biting. I do think that in a way she went crazy.

Two men held Hatsumomo from behind as she struggled and kicked and screamed. Unnoticed by anybody, Mameha left and returned a moment later with the mistress of the teahouse. The mistress and Shojiro threw Hatsumomo out of the party.

Hatsumomo didn't return to the *okiya* at all that night. When she did come back the following day, she smelled like she'd been sick and her hair was all over the place. Mother took her into her room and she was there a long time.

A few days later Hatsumomo left the *okiya* and never came back. She was wearing a simple cotton dress Mother had given her and her hair was long, down to her shoulders. I'd never seen it like that before. She didn't leave voluntarily; Mother had thrown her out. Hatsumomo wasn't earning what she once had, and Mameha believed that Mother had wanted to get rid of her for years.

Chapter 10   World War II

Having General Tottori as my *danna* brought little change to my life. But his help to the *okiya* was extremely useful, at least from Mother's point of view. He paid for many of my expenses, as a *danna* usually does—including the cost of my lessons, my annual registration fee at the school, my medical expenses and ... Oh, I don't even know what else—my socks probably.

But more importantly, his job with the army was everything Mameha had said it would be. For example, Mother grew sick during March of 1939. We were terribly worried about her and the doctors were no help. But after a telephone call to the General, an important doctor from the military hospital called and gave Mother some medicine that cured her.

The General sent regular deliveries of tea and sugar, as well as some luxuries like make-up and chocolates, which were becoming scarce even in Gion. And of course, Mother had been quite wrong about the war ending within six months. We couldn't believe it at the time but we'd hardly seen the beginning of the dark years.

In Japan we refer to the years of the Depression through World War II as *kuraitani*—the valley of darkness. In Gion we never suffered as much as others. While most Japanese lived in this dark valley all through the 1930s, for example, in Gion we were still warmed by a bit of sun. And because of General Tottori the sun still reached us, even in World War II.

At least, it reached us until one afternoon just a few weeks before New Year's Day, in December 1942. I'd been busy helping to clean the *okiya* in preparation for the New Year. I was eating my lunch when a man's voice called out at our entrance. Mother spoke to him and then spoke hurriedly to me. "General Tottori was arrested this morning," she said. "You'd better hide our best things, or they'll be gone tomorrow."

Within a week we were no longer the people who helped all their friends; instead we were the people who most needed help. We'd always got tea for Mameha, but now she began to get it for us.

One day soon the geisha districts would close and we feared we would all end up in factories. We all knew geisha who were already there. Hatsumomo's tall friend, for example, the geisha Korin. She was in a Tokyo factory working double shifts with only a bowl of weak soup with a bit of potato in it for food every day.

Then one morning in the January of 1943, I was standing in line at the rice store in the falling snow, when the shopkeeper next door put out his head and called into the cold:

"It's happened!"

We all looked at each other. For a moment I was too cold to care what he meant. I had thin peasants' clothing on; no one wore a kimono during the day any longer. Finally the geisha in front of me wiped some snow from her face and asked the shopkeeper what he meant.

"The government has announced the closing of the geisha district," he said. "All of you must report to the registry office tomorrow morning for factory work."

I looked at the desperation on the faces of the other geisha around me and I knew we were all thinking the same thing: Which of the men we knew could save us from life in the factories?

There was a rumor that General Tottori had been released and was living in the Suruya Inn, the same place where we'd met during the evenings for so many years. Even though the General had been my *danna* until the previous year, I certainly wasn't the only geisha who knew him. I had to reach him before anybody else did.

I wasn't dressed for the weather, but I started at once for the northwest of the city. I arrived there an hour or two later, red with the cold and covered with snow. But when I greeted the mistress of the inn, she took a long look at me before bowing in apology and saying she had no idea who I was.

"It's me . . . Sayuri. I've come to speak with the General."

"Sayuri-san! I never thought I'd see you looking like the wife of a peasant."

She led me inside at once, but before she took me to the General, she dressed me in one of her kimonos. She even found some make-up she had hidden and put it on me, so the General would know who I was.

When I entered his room, General Tottori was sitting at the table listening to the radio. I could see in his face and on his thin body how hard the past years had been for him. He'd been accused of some awful crimes, including theft; some people thought he was lucky not to be in prison. I read an attack on him in a magazine that said that the Japanese Navy's defeat in the South Pacific was all his fault because the supplies were so bad.

"You're looking very well, General," I said, though of course this was a lie. "What a pleasure it is to see you again!"

The General switched off the radio. "You're not the first

person to come to me," he said. "There's nothing I can do to help you, Sayuri."

"But I rushed here so quickly! I can't imagine how anyone reached you before I did!"

"Since last week nearly every geisha I know has been to see me, but I don't have friends in power any longer. I don't know why a top geisha like you should come to me anyway. You're liked by so many men with influence."

"There is a difference between being popular and having real friends who will help," I said.

"Yes, you're right. What sort of help have you come to me for anyway?"

"Any help at all, General. We talk about nothing these days in Gion except how miserable life in a factory will be."

"Life will be miserable for the lucky ones. The rest won't even live to see the end of the war."

"I don't understand."

"The bombs will fall soon," the General said. "You can be certain the factories will receive more than their share. If you want to be alive when this war is over, you'd better find someone who can put you in a safe place. I'm sorry I'm not that man, Sayuri. I've already used any influence I had."

The General asked about Mother's health and then we said good-bye. I learned only much later what he meant about using all his influence. The mistress of the Suruya had a young daughter; the General had arranged to send her to a town in northern Japan.

I went to see Mameha. She was nearly as frightened as I was. Her relationship with her *danna*, the Baron, had ended, and she was now living in a much smaller apartment. She had no advice for me because she was unable to help herself.

"The Baron will do nothing to help me," she said, her face pale with worry. "I've been unable to reach the other men I have in mind. You had better think of someone, Sayuri, and go to him as quickly as you can."

Of course I thought of the Chairman. I would have taken any chance just to speak to him. But I could never have asked him for a favor. He was warm to me when we met by chance, but I wasn't invited to Iwamura parties even when lesser geisha were. I felt hurt by this, but what could I do?

But even if the Chairman had wanted to help me, his problems with the military government had been in the newspapers lately. He had too many of his own troubles.

So I spent the rest of that afternoon going from teahouse to teahouse in the biting cold, asking about men I hadn't seen in weeks or even months. None of the mistresses knew where to find them.

◆

Just before General Tottori became my *danna*, Nobu used to watch me at the Ichiriki Teahouse, looking more and more puzzled. He'd expected to arrange everything with Mother quickly and to become my *danna*. I expected that myself, at the time. Even the mistress of the Ichiriki was worried by how angry Nobu was when it didn't happen. I remember him at a party, walking past the mistress without looking at her, his jaw shut hard in anger. And I'll never forget his angry eyes, watching me all through the evening while guests at the party were laughing and enjoying themselves. That was the last time I'd seen him, over four years ago.

That evening, the Ichiriki had a last party before it closed. Some of the geisha looked half dead with fear; others looked calm and lovely, painted with just a little sadness.

I don't know how I looked. My mind was working all the time, thinking which man I'd talk to and how I'd do it. I hardly heard a maid tell me I was wanted in another room. I imagined a group of men had requested my company, but the maid led me to the small rooms at the back of the teahouse. She opened the door of a small *tatami* room I'd never entered before. And there at the table, alone with a glass of beer, sat Nobu.

There was a beer for me too. Beer was very unusual at this time. When the maid had left, I sat down at the table and we raised our glasses.

"Here's a drink to your *danna*," said Nobu. "Four years ago I told you he wasn't good enough for you and I was right. Don't you agree?"

"The truth is . . . he isn't my *danna* any longer."

"Exactly! And even if he were, he couldn't do a thing for you, could he? Gion's going to close and everyone's terrified for their lives. I received a call at my office today from a certain geisha . . . I won't name her. She asked if I could find her a job at Iwamura Electric."

"If you don't mind me asking, what did you tell her?"

"I don't have a job for anyone, hardly even myself. Even the Chairman may have no job soon. He'll be in prison if he doesn't do what the government says. They want us to make airplanes! I mean, honestly! Iwamura make refrigerators and heaters. Sometimes I ask myself what these people are thinking."

"Nobu-san should speak more quietly."

"Who's going to hear me? Your General?"

"Speaking of the General," I said, "I did go to see him today, to ask for his help."

"He didn't help you, did he?"

"No, he said he'd already used the influence he had."

"That wouldn't have taken him long. Why didn't he save his influence for you?"

"I haven't seen him in more than a year . . ."

"You haven't seen me in more than four years. And I *have* saved my best influence for you. Why didn't you come to me before now?"

"Because I imagined you were angry with me all this time. Just look at you, Nobu-san. Look at the anger in your face. How could I have come to you?"

"How could you *not* come? I can save you from the factories. I have something perfect for you. Just like a nest for a bird. You're the only one I'll give it to, Sayuri. But I won't give it until you've bowed to the floor and admitted how wrong you were, when you took General Tottori as your *danna*. Oh yes, I'm angry with you!"

I did what Nobu asked of me. I moved away from the table to make room, and I bowed low to the floor.

"Forgive me for my foolishness," I said.

◆

All the kimono-makers were now making parachutes because they were used to working with silk. Nobu had arranged for me to stay with one of them, a family called Arashino. They lived in the country, outside Kyoto.

The Arashinos were very kind to me during the years I lived in their home. By day I worked with them, sewing parachutes. At night I slept next to their daughter and grandson on a futon on the floor of the workshop where we made the parachutes.

Of course, there wasn't much food. You can't imagine some of the things we learned to eat. We ate food that was usually given to animals. And there was something called *nukapan* that looked like old dry leather, though the leather would probably have tasted better.

I grew so thin during those years that nobody would have recognized me on the streets of Gion. Some days the Arashinos' little grandson, Juntaro, cried from hunger—and then Mr. Arashino sold one of the kimonos he used to make. This was what we Japanese called the "onion life"—removing layer after layer, and crying all the time.

71

One night in the spring of 1944 we saw the first bombs dropped on Japan. The bombers passed over us, not only that night but every night. They were flying to the factories in Osaka and Tokyo. I was desperately worried about the Chairman and Nobu, working at the Iwamura factory in Osaka.

The Kamo River flowed below our workshop before it ran to Osaka and then out into the sea. Day after day I threw flowers into the river, hoping that the Chairman, sitting at his desk in Osaka, might look out of the window and see them and think of me.

But even if he saw the flowers, I feared he wouldn't think of me. He'd often been kind to me, it was true, but he was a kind man. He'd never shown any sign of recognizing that I was the girl on the bridge or that I cared for him or thought of him.

If I came to the end of my life and had spent every day watching for a man who never came to me, what life would I have had? I'd be like a dancer who had practiced since childhood for a performance she would never give.

◆

I learned during those years that nothing is as unpredictable as who will survive a war and who won't. Mameha survived, working as a nurse in a small hospital, but her maid, Asami, was killed by the terrible bomb that fell on Nagasaki.

Some of the people in the most dangerous places survived. Hatsumomo's dresser, Mr. Bekku, who had taken me from my home in Yoroido, worked for the navy in Osaka and survived somehow. Pumpkin worked in a factory in Osaka that was bombed five times, but she also survived. So did General Tottori, who lived in the Suruya Inn until his death in the mid-1950s. But the geisha Korin and Katsue and the wrestler Miyagiyama were all killed by firebombs in Tokyo.

There was never any doubt that Mother would survive. She

spent the war buying and selling, growing richer not poorer. When Mr. Arashino needed to sell a kimono, who do you think bought it from him? And then sold it again for much more than she paid for it.

The war ended for us in August of 1945. Almost everyone who lived in Japan at this time will tell you that it was the blackest moment in a long night of darkness. For a year or more I never once heard the sound of laughter.

But by the spring of 1946 there was again talk of Japan's rebirth. All the stories about American soldiers killing us were shown to be wrong; the Americans were extremely kind. As they drove past on trucks, throwing candy to our children, they had no eyes for me: a thin woman in worn peasant clothes, with hands rough from work on the parachutes. But why had we been taught to hate them?

One cold November afternoon, three years after the end of the war, Mr. Arashino told me there was somebody to see me. By this time Mr. Arashino was making kimonos again and I was helping him.

My visitor was Nobu. He told me that Gion was open again.

Chapter 11   Nobu Again

"I have a task for you to do in Gion," said Nobu. "If it works out as I hope, our company will be trading again in a year or two. Then the time will have come at last for me to become your *danna*."

My skin went cold when I heard this, but I showed no sign of it. "How mysterious, Nobu-san. A task *I* could do, which would be helpful to Iwamura Electric?"

"It's an awful task. I won't lie to you. I want you to entertain a man called Sato. He looks and behaves like a pig. He tells me he always sat across the table so he could stare at you. You're the only thing he ever talks about—when he talks at all; most of the time he just sits."

I had to laugh when I heard this. "How awful a task can that be? However much Nobu-san dislikes him, I'm sure I've entertained worse. But how would that help Iwamura?"

Nobu sighed. "All through the war, the Chairman resisted the government's orders. When he finally agreed to cooperate, the war was almost over, and nothing we ever made for them—not one thing—was used in the war. But now we have to prove that to the Americans. If they don't believe us, they will take Iwamura, sell it, and use the money to help victims of the war. Sato is the man who will make the decision about Iwamura for the Americans. He's the new Deputy Minister of Finance."

"Nobu-san," I said, "if it's important to make a good impression on Deputy Minister Sato, maybe you should ask the Chairman to be there when you entertain him."

"The Chairman is a busy man. Sayuri, you do look like a peasant."

And then Nobu got up and left.

The next day I said a tearful good-bye to the Arashinos and, at the age of nearly thirty, I went back to Gion. Mother and I spent four or five days cleaning the *okiya*, helped by one cook, one maid, and a girl called Etsuko. She was the daughter of the man who owned the farm where Mother had lived during the war. Etsuko was twelve, the same age as I was when I first came to Kyoto.

When the *okiya* was clean, I went to see Mameha. She was now in a one-room apartment near the Gion Shrine. She was shocked when she first saw me because I was so thin. The truth was, I was just as shocked at the changes in her. Her face was still as lovely as ever, but her neck looked too old for her face. Her mouth showed the problems she'd had with her teeth during the war.

74

We talked for a long time, and then I asked her if she thought *Dances of the Old Capital* would start again, the following spring. It hadn't been performed for a number of years.

"With all the American soldiers in Gion these days," she said, "English will get you further than dance. Anyway, the Kaburenjo Theater has been turned into an American cabaret. There's even a new Japanese word for it—*kyaberei*."

About a week after my return, I was finally ready to make my first appearance as a geisha again. Since I was nearing thirty, I would no longer be expected to wear white make-up except on special occasions. But I did spend half an hour trying western-style make-up to try to hide how thin I'd become.

When Mr. Bekku came to dress me, young Etsuko stood and watched just as I'd once watched Hatsumomo. It was the astonishment in her eyes, more than anything I saw while looking in the mirror, that persuaded me I truly looked like a geisha again.

When at last I set out that evening, snow covered Gion. There were soldiers here and there on the streets and I didn't want to think about what I might find when I reached the Ichiriki. But the only differences were the black shoes of the officers in the entrance, and strangely enough the teahouse was quieter than before the war.

I waited for Nobu and Deputy Minister Sato in an empty room next to the room where I would entertain them. No geisha likes to be seen doing nothing; it makes her look unpopular. This gave me a chance to listen to Nobu struggling to be pleasant as he brought the Minister in.

"Isn't this a nice room, Minister?" said Nobu. I heard a grunt in reply. The Minister really did sound like a pig. Nobu continued, "It's a beautiful night, isn't it? Did I already ask you if you tasted the Ichiriki Teahouse's own special *sake*?"

When I left my empty room and joined Nobu and the Deputy Minister, Nobu looked very pleased to see me.

I got my first good look at the Minister only after introducing myself and going to kneel at the table. I didn't remember him, even if he *had* said he'd spent hours staring at me. He kept his chin down on his chest and made no sound except grunts.

When the maid arrived with *sake*, the Minister poured the drink directly into his lower jaw. He didn't seem to swallow it at all but it disappeared like water down a drain.

Things went on like this for about fifteen minutes; the Minister grunted and poured *sake* into his jaw. Then he finally said something. He asked me if I was a dancer.

"Yes! Yes, I am," I said. "Would the Minister like me to perform a short dance?"

"No," he said. And that was the end of that.

Very soon we began to play a drinking game. The Minister had never played it before. He kept losing, kept drinking, and Nobu and I just got him out to the snow-covered garden before he threw up. Then the Minister lay very still on his back in the snow.

"Well, Nobu-san," I said. "I didn't know how much fun your guest was going to be."

"I believe we've killed him."

"You must take him out into the street and walk him around a bit to wake him up. The cold will do him good."

"He's lying in the snow. Isn't that cold enough?"

"Nobu-san!" I said.

I went to get a maid to help because Nobu couldn't get the Minister on his feet with only one arm. With the maid's help we got the Minister back inside. The maid cleaned the Minister's jacket and left us alone again.

"We need more geisha next time," I said to Nobu, above the sleeping Minister. "And maybe you should bring the Chairman next time too."

The Minister opened his eyes and managed to pull himself up a little.

"Well, Minister, this certainly has been a wonderful evening!" said Nobu. "Next time we'll have even more fun. Instead of throwing up on just me, you might be able to throw up on the Chairman, and maybe another geisha or two as well!"

"I like this geisha," said the Minister. "I don't want another one."

Whatever the Minister said, it was obvious that we needed more geisha next time. I'd ask Mameha, of course, but I wanted to ask Pumpkin too.

I knew almost nothing about Pumpkin's circumstances, except that she was back in Gion, so I went to speak with Mother. Mother told me that Pumpkin had asked to come back to the *okiya* when it had reopened but that she, Mother, had refused because Pumpkin would be a poor investment.

"She's living in a poor little *okiya* over in the Hanami-cho area," Mother said. "But don't go and see her. I think it would be foolish of you to speak with her."

"I have to admit," I said, "I've never felt right about what happened between Pumpkin and me . . ."

"Nothing happened between you. Pumpkin didn't do well enough and you succeeded. Anyway, she's doing better these days. The Americans can't get enough of her. She says exactly what she thinks. The Americans like that."

That afternoon I crossed Shijo Avenue to the Hanami-cho area of Gion, and found the poor little *okiya* Mother had told me about. A young maid showed me into a room that didn't smell too good, and came back later to bring me a cup of weak tea. I waited a long time before Pumpkin at last came and slid open the door.

I felt such warmth for her. I got up from the table, wanting to put my arms around her. She took a few steps into the room and then knelt and gave a formal bow, as if I was Mother. I didn't know what to do and just stopped in the middle of the room.

"Really, Pumpkin . . . it's only me!" I said.

She wouldn't even look at me, but looked down at the mats like a maid waiting for orders. I felt very disappointed and went back to my place at the table.

When we'd last seen each other, during the war, Pumpkin's face was still round and full, but now her heavy cheeks had thinned, leaving her with an elegance that was astonishing to me. I don't mean that Pumpkin had suddenly become a beauty like Hatsumomo, but her face had a certain womanliness that had never been there before.

It was a long time later that I found out what had happened to Pumpkin. After the closing of the factory where she worked, she had to spend more than two years in Osaka, on the streets, selling herself.

"I'm sure the years have been difficult, Pumpkin," I said to her, "but you look quite lovely."

Pumpkin didn't reply to this. She just moved her head to show that she'd heard me. I congratulated her on her popularity and tried asking about her life since the war, but her face showed no expression, so I began to feel sorry I'd come.

Finally, after an awkward silence, she spoke.

"Have you come here just to chat, Sayuri? Because I don't have anything to say that will interest you."

"The truth is," I said, "I saw Nobu Toshikazu recently, and . . . actually Pumpkin, he'll be bringing Deputy Minister Sato to Gion sometimes. I thought you'd be kind enough to help us entertain him."

"I know you think I'm stupid . . ."

"Pumpkin!"

"But you probably have some other reason you're not going to tell me about."

"I suppose I do have another reason," I said. "To tell the truth,

I'd hoped that after all these years, you and I might be friends, as we once were. We've survived so many things together... including Hatsumomo!"

Pumpkin said nothing.

However, she accepted her invitation to the Ichiriki that Saturday, and she and Mameha and I entertained the Chairman, Nobu, and Sato all through that winter and the following spring, once or twice a week, as long as Sato was deciding the future of Iwamura Electric.

Pumpkin was very good with Sato. The first time she met him she said, in the direct way she now had, "Hey, Minister, I'll bet you don't remember me, but I know a lot about you."

"What do you know?" said Mameha. "Tell us something."

"I know the Minister has a younger sister who's married to the mayor of Tokyo," Pumpkin said. "And I know he broke his hand in a fight once."

The Minister was looking surprised, so these things must have been true. But Pumpkin wasn't finished yet.

"Also Minister, I know a girl you used to know, Nau Itsuko. We worked in a factory outside Osaka together. You know what she told me? She told me you and she did some bad, bad things together."

I was afraid the Minister might be angry, but he looked quite proud of himself. He and Pumpkin were soon friendly, and the Chairman seemed to like her too.

Pumpkin wore a really extraordinary gray kimono to the parties, with bright gold dots on it. These were stars set against a background of water and mountains, in the light of the moon. Neither my kimono nor Mameha's could compare with it.

The Chairman seemed to like the kimono too because he asked Pumpkin to model it for him. She turned around and around slowly for him, so that he could admire her. At the next party Pumpkin wasn't there, she was sick, and the Chairman left early. I spent many unhappy hours wondering if these two events were connected.

My concern about the Chairman's opinion of me made me take a chance. We were playing a game called "Truth and Lies." You have to tell two stories. One of them is the truth, and the other a lie—and then everyone guesses which one was which. Geisha play this game so often that they all have lots of stories ready. But this time I told a story that I'd never told before.

"Once when I was a child," I began, "I was very upset one day, and I went to the banks of the Shirakawa Stream and began to cry . . ."

As I began this story, I felt almost as though I were reaching across the table to touch the Chairman on the hand. It seemed to me that no one else in the room would consider the story to be unusual, but the Chairman would understand it—or at least I hoped he would. I felt I was having a very private conversation with him alone, and I could feel myself getting warm as I spoke.

When I finished my story, I looked up, expecting to find the Chairman looking at me with understanding, but he didn't even seem to be listening. I felt a fool. Like a girl who walks along the street imagining that every man is looking at her, but the street is empty.

Luckily, the Minister was too drunk to notice anything, and Nobu was busy eating his food. Mameha had just started her story. Pumpkin, though, had been watching me carefully. When I looked at her, she had a smile on her face that I feared, though I didn't completely understand it.

Worse followed. Minister Sato had asked the mistress of the Ichiriki if he could be my *danna*. Nobu and Mother together didn't have too much difficulty in stopping this. They told the mistress of the Ichiriki to tell Sato that I wasn't available.

Nobu was telling me what happened next. He looked angry,

even for him. "And do you know what that foolish Minister Sato said? After he found out he wasn't going to be your *danna*, he sat there for a long time like a pile of dirt and then he finally said, 'Could you arrange for me to be Sayuri's *danna* just once?' He meant for one night! Really! You wouldn't do that, would you?"

"Nobu-san . . ."

"If you're a woman who would do such a thing, I want you to leave this room right now, and never speak to me again!"

He picked his beer glass up and banged it down again on the table so hard that it cracked and beer spilled on the table. He'd cut his hand on the glass too, and there was blood on it. I couldn't understand how the evening had suddenly become so dangerous; but it was perfectly clear to me that I could give only one answer.

"I would never do that," I said.

I thought that would calm him, but for a long terrifying moment the anger stayed in his face. Then he slowly breathed out.

"Next time, speak before I have to cut myself for an answer," he said. "Now listen. Things are possible that weren't possible before. Sato is going to tell the Americans the truth, that Iwamura didn't help the government in the war. The Chairman and I are safe now. I'm going to be your *danna*."

I left the room as quickly as I could to find a maid to help with Nobu's hand, which was covered with blood from his cut.

Chapter 12   Sato

That night as I lay on my futon, I decided to be like a fisherman who hour after hour takes out fish from his net. Whenever I thought of the Chairman, I took the thought from my mind and then again and again until no thoughts were left. It would have been a good system, I'm sure, if I could have made it work. I even tried to think of Nobu instead of the Chairman, but without success.

I did this for weeks, trying to remake myself. I went to parties as usual, but I knelt in silence with my hands in my lap. Mother told me I looked like a ghost. She'd brought in a newspaper while I was eating lunch. There was an article in it about Iwamura. It was a difficult article to read, full of numbers and business terms. But it was clear that Iwamura could make their heaters and refrigerators again, and in the same week the company had got a big loan from Mitsubishi Bank.

"It's no wonder we've heard so much from Nobu Toshikazu these past few days," said Mother. "You must know he wants to be your *danna*. Well, there's no problem with that now. It's finally happening. We all know how fond you've been of Nobu these past few years."

Mother followed this with some news. The mistress of the Ichiriki had received a telephone call that morning from Iwamura Electric about a trip to the island of Amami, the following weekend. I'd been asked to go, with Mameha and Pumpkin. We were going by airplane. I'd never been on one—I'd never even seen one. I was terrified.

♦

When Friday morning came, we started for Osaka by train. In addition to Mr. Bekku, who came as far as the airport to help us with our trunks, the little group consisted of Mameha, Pumpkin, and me.

From Osaka Station we traveled to the airport in a little bus not much larger than a car, which burned coal and was very dirty. At last, after an hour or more, we climbed down beside a silver airplane balanced on tiny wheels; and when we went inside the airplane sloped down so much I thought it was broken.

The men were there already, sitting in seats at the back.

With the Chairman, Nobu, and Minister Sato, there was an elderly man who I later learned was President of the Mitsubishi Bank.

We sat toward the front of the airplane and left the men to their dull conversation. Soon I heard a coughing noise and the airplane shook. Then it started to move. The noise of the engines grew worse, and the airplane began to move forward. Finally the noise grew to a terrifying roar, and we began to rise up into the air.

Mameha had put me in a window seat, thinking the view might calm me, but now she saw the ground disappearing below us and she refused to switch seats with me. Someone finally told me the trip was seven hundred kilometers and would take nearly four hours, but only when the ground was far below us. When I heard this, I'm afraid tears came into my eyes, and everyone began to laugh at me.

I pulled the curtains over the windows and tried to calm myself by reading a magazine. Some time later, after Mameha had fallen asleep in the seat beside me, I looked up and saw Nobu standing over me.

"Sayuri, are you well?" he said, speaking quietly so he didn't wake Mameha.

"I don't think Nobu-san has ever asked me that before," I said. "He must be in a very cheerful mood."

"The future has never looked better!"

Nobu looked at me and then walked away. For a moment I thought he might see in my eyes that I was as worried about my future with him as he was happy about his future with me. But of course he didn't. Nobu understood me so little. A geisha who expects understanding from her *danna* is like a mouse expecting sympathy from a snake.

The Chairman was the only man I'd ever entertained as Sayuri the geisha who had also known me as Chiyo. Why couldn't I stop thinking about the Chairman? If you'd asked me that, I would have answered, "Why does water run downhill?" "Why do fish taste of fish?"

I looked out of the airplane window at the blue water far below. And then a frightening picture came into my mind of me cutting the cord that tied me to Nobu and watching him fall from the airplane into the ocean.

Of course, I don't mean that I was really going to throw Nobu out of the airplane, but I did have a sudden understanding of the one thing I could do to end my relationship with him forever. Nobu himself had told me how to do it, just a moment after cutting his hand that night at the Ichiriki Teahouse only a few weeks earlier. If I could agree to give myself to Minister Sato for one night, he'd said, he would never speak to me again.

As we left the airplane, I must still have looked very worried because Mameha kept telling me that I was safe at last.

◆

We arrived at our inn about an hour before sunset. The others admired the room where we would all be staying. I pretended to admire it too, but I wasn't really interested; I was too worried about what I was going to do. But the room *was* nice. It was as big as the largest room at the Ichiriki Teahouse, with *tatami* mats, dark wood and beautiful Japanese furniture.

When the luggage was unpacked, we were all ready for a bath. The men's and women's changing and washing areas were separate, but when we entered the pool of natural water at the inn we were together. In my day it was considered normal for geisha to take a bath with their best customers and sleep in the same room as them.

A geisha would never be alone with a man who wasn't her *danna*, but in a group like this, with water covering our bodies, well, that was accepted. And we even have a word for sleeping in a group—*zakone*, "fish sleeping." If you picture in your mind the way fish look in a basket, you'll understand the name.

Nobu had been in the water for a long time, talking to the Chairman, but now he was sitting on a rock with only his legs in the water. He was rubbing the stump of his arm with the other hand and looking into the water.

I'd never seen his body before. His damaged shoulder looked as bad as his face. And now I was thinking about betraying him. He'd think I'd done it for only one reason, and would never understand the truth. I hated the thought of hurting Nobu or destroying his good opinion of me. Could I really do what I'd thought of on the airplane?

♦

After breakfast the following morning, we all took a walk through the streets of the little village. Nobu was as cheerful as I'd ever seen him. We found an old wood building with a sloped roof. We walked around to the back, where Nobu climbed stone steps to open a door at the corner. Sunlight fell across a dusty stage built out of wood; at one time this had obviously been the town's theater.

I had a picture in my mind of me lying there on that wooden stage with Minister Sato as the door opened and sunlight fell on us. We'd have no place to hide; Nobu couldn't possibly fail to see us.

As we walked back toward our inn, I walked behind the rest of the group because I wanted to take my handkerchief from my sleeve. It was very hot and the sun was shining full onto our faces. Nobu came walking back to ask if I was all right.

"You haven't looked well all weekend, Sayuri," he said. "Maybe you should have stayed in Kyoto."

"But then I wouldn't have seen this beautiful island."

"I'm sure this is the farthest you've ever been from your home. We're a long way from Kyoto now."

I had the same thought that I'd had on the airplane; that Nobu didn't understand me at all. Kyoto wasn't my home. And at that moment, as I looked at him in the hot sun, I decided to betray Nobu, even though he was looking at me with kindness.

But I had no idea how I'd get Minister Sato to the theater with me, and even less idea how I'd arrange for Nobu to find us there. Maybe Pumpkin would take Nobu for a walk if I asked her to? I didn't think I could ask Mameha. Pumpkin would be much less shocked at what I was planning than Mameha would be. I'd need to tell Pumpkin very clearly to bring Nobu to the old theater.

But first I had to speak to the Minister, who right now was putting fish into his lower jaw. He ate in the same way as he drank beer. It looked awful.

"Minister," I said, "when you have finished your food why don't you and I look around the inn together?"

I didn't wait for him to reply, but walked from the room. I was relieved when he came out a moment later to join me.

"Minister," I said, "why don't we take a walk back down to the village together?"

He looked very confused by this.

"There's something I would like to see again," I added.

The Minister grunted a "yes" and I told him to wait while I went to find Pumpkin. She was in her room, looking through her trunk for something.

"Pumpkin," I said, "I need to ask a favor."

I waited for her to tell me she was happy to help, but she just stood with her eyes on me.

"I hope you won't mind me asking . . ."

"Ask," she said.

"The Minister and I are going for a walk. I'm going to take him to the old theater, and . . ."

"Why?"

"So that he and I can be alone."

"You want to be *alone*? With the *Minister*? Are you crazy?"

"I'll explain some other time, but this is what I want you to do. I want you to bring Nobu there and . . . Pumpkin, this will sound very strange. I want you to find us there together."

"What game are you playing, Sayuri?"

"I don't have time to explain it now. But it's terribly important, Pumpkin. Truthfully, my entire future is in your hands. Just make sure that Nobu sees me and the Minister together. I'll repay you in any way you like."

She looked at me for a long moment. "So it's time for a favor from Pumpkin again, is it?" she said.

As I walked back to the village with the Minister, I remembered the day Mameha had cut me on the leg and taken me to see Dr. Crab. On that afternoon I'd felt in some sort of danger I couldn't fully understand, and I felt much the same way now. But I kept talking in the hot sun as we walked all the way back to the theater.

"Will you come inside with me for a moment, Minister?"

He didn't seem to know how to react to this, but when I climbed the stone steps and went into the theater he walked after me. But then he just stood there, like a man waiting for a bus.

My hands were shaking. I didn't know if I could do what I'd planned to do.

"Minister," I said. "Even if you can't be my *danna* . . ."

A look of understanding spread slowly across the Minister's face.

"We'll go over there," he said, pointing to a corner of the theater.

That was no good. Nobu could miss us if we lay in a corner.

"Let's go up on the stage," I said.

I lay down on the stage, and the Minister lay down on top of me. When he touched me, I imagined life with Nobu as my *danna* and that helped me to let him do what he wanted. With his jaw on top of my face he looked more animal than human. I shut my eyes.

And then the door opened and there was sunlight over us as we lay there. With the Minister on top of me I had to look carefully but I could just recognize two people. One of them was Pumpkin. The other one was the Chairman.

Chapter 13   The Chairman

Mameha was kneeling above me. I was puzzled to find that I wasn't in the old theater any longer, but looking up from the *tatami* floor of a dark little room at the inn. I didn't remember leaving the theater, but I must have done it somehow.

Later, as I walked unsteadily back to my room with a terrible feeling of fear, I saw Pumpkin just coming out of her room. She stopped when she saw me; but she didn't apologize as I half-expected. She turned her head slowly and looked at me the way a snake might look at a mouse.

"Pumpkin," I said, "I asked you to bring Nobu, not the Chairman. I don't understand . . ."

"Yes, it must be difficult for you to understand, Sayuri, when life doesn't work out perfectly!"

"Perfectly? Nothing worse could have happened . . . did you misunderstand what I was asking you?"

"You really do think I'm stupid!" she said.

I was confused, and just stood there in silence. "I thought you were my friend," I said at last.

"I thought you were my friend too, once. But that was a long time ago."

"You talk as if I'd done something to harm you, Pumpkin, but . . ."

"No, you'd never do anything like that, would you? Not the perfect Miss Nitta Sayuri! I suppose it doesn't matter that you took my place as daughter of the *okiya*? Do you remember that, Sayuri? After I'd helped you about the Doctor—whatever his name was. After I'd risked making Hatsumomo mad at me for helping you! After all that, you stole what was mine."

"But Pumpkin," I interrupted, "couldn't you just have refused to help me? Why did you have to bring the Chairman?"

She looked me in the eye. "I know perfectly well how you feel about him," she said. "Whenever you think there's nobody looking, you look at him like you were his dog. You took something from me a long time ago, Sayuri. Well, how does it feel now?"

During the rest of that evening I don't remember anything very clearly; while the others were drinking and laughing, I could only pretend to laugh. I must have been red because from time to time Mameha touched my neck to see if I was feverish.

I sat as far away from the Chairman as I could, so that our eyes wouldn't have to meet; and I did survive the evening without talking to him. But later, as we were all getting ready for bed, I passed the Chairman as he was going into his room. I should have moved out of his way, but I felt too ashamed. I gave a quick bow and hurried past him, not even trying to hide how unhappy I felt.

After everyone else was asleep, I left the inn with my head spinning and walked back to the ocean. It was dark, the wind was screaming, and the waves were crashing angrily. It was as though the wind and the water had taken on the spirit of my old girlhood enemy, Hatsumomo.

The screaming of the wind and the crashing of the waves seemed to laugh at me. Could it really be that the stream of my life had turned away from the Chairman forever? I took his handkerchief from my sleeve. I'd taken it to bed with me that evening as usual and then put it in my sleeve when I went out. I dried my face with it and then held it up into the wind.

I thought of letting it go and letting the wind take it, but then I thought of the letter Mr. Tanaka had sent me so many years earlier, telling me that my parents were dead. We must always keep something to remember those who have left us. The letter was all that remained of my childhood. The Chairman's handkerchief would be what remained of the rest of my life.

◆

On Wednesday morning, only three days after our return from Amami, I got a message that someone from Iwamura Electric had telephoned the Ichiriki Teahouse to request my presence that evening. This could only mean that everything was still all right after the events on Amami, and Nobu was ready to become my *danna*.

I dressed late in the afternoon in a yellow silk kimono with a green underskirt and a dark blue and gold *obi*. I looked at myself in the mirror and saw a defeated woman. My face looked thin, even though as usual I'd put on western-style make-up; even my hair didn't look right. I couldn't think of any way to improve my appearance except to ask Mr. Bekku to re-tie my *obi* a little higher, to take away some of my sad look.

At the Ichiriki, a maid took me upstairs to the same room where Nobu had met with me on the night Gion was closing. This must mean that Nobu wanted us to meet in the same room to celebrate becoming my *danna*—though it wouldn't be a celebration for me. But it would be a fine night for Nobu and I would try not to spoil it.

I knelt at one end of the table, careful to position myself so that Nobu could pour *sake* using his one arm. Could it really be that only five and a half years had passed since our last evening together in this room? So many people had come and gone; so many people I'd once known were now dead.

Was this the life I'd come back to Gion to lead? It was just as Mameha had once told me: we don't become geisha because we want our lives to be happy; we become geisha because we have no choice. If my mother had lived, I might be a wife and mother in Yoroido, by the sea, thinking of Kyoto as a faraway place where the fish were sent.

After ten or fifteen minutes waiting for Nobu, I began to wonder if he was really coming. I knew I shouldn't do it but I lay my head down on the table to rest. I'd slept badly these last few nights.

I didn't fall asleep, but I lost myself for a time in my sadness. And then I had a dream. I dreamt that I felt the Chairman's hand touching my shoulder. I knew it was the Chairman's hand because when I opened my eyes he was there.

For a moment I wondered if I was really awake; but it wasn't a dream. The Chairman was sitting exactly where I'd expected Nobu to sit.

"Nobu-san is . . . quite all right, is he?" I said.

"Oh yes," said the Chairman. "Quite all right. But he won't be coming this evening."

I was relieved to hear this; but at the same time I was ashamed. I remembered how the Chairman had seen me on Amami, with Minister Sato on top of me with his pants down.

"May I please say, Chairman," I began as steadily as I could, "that my behavior on Amami . . ."

"I know what you're thinking, Sayuri. But I haven't come here to ask for your apology. Sit quietly a moment. I want to tell you about something that happened a long time ago."

"Chairman, I feel so confused," I managed to say. "Please forgive me, but . . ."

"Just listen," said the Chairman. "One day, eighteen years ago, I was with a geisha and some friends, taking a walk by the Shirakawa Stream on our way to the theater."

I took the Chairman's handkerchief from my *obi* and silently put it on the table.

"Where did you get this?"

"Chairman," I said, "all these years I've wondered if you knew I was the little girl you'd spoken to. You gave me your handkerchief on the way to see the play *Shibaraku*."

"Do you mean to say ... even when you were an apprentice, you knew that I was the man who'd spoken to you?"

"I recognized the Chairman the moment I saw him again at the *sumo* exhibition. But I'm amazed the Chairman remembered *me*."

"Well, maybe you should look at yourself in the mirror sometimes, Sayuri. Your eyes ... I can't explain it. I spend so much of my time talking to men who are never quite telling me the truth; and here was a girl who let me look into her eyes and see straight into her."

And then the Chairman interrupted himself.

"Didn't you ever wonder why Mameha became your Older Sister?" he asked me.

"Mameha? What does Mameha have to do with all this?"

"Sayuri, I am the one who asked Mameha to look after you. I told her about a beautiful young girl I'd met, with amazing gray eyes. I asked her to help you if she ever met you in Gion. And she did meet you. It was two years later, but Mameha remembered. You would certainly never have become a geisha without her help."

It's almost impossible to describe the effect the Chairman's words had on me. I'd always thought that Mameha's reason for helping me was personal—to get rid of Hatsumomo because she hated her. So Mameha was suddenly a different woman in my eyes, and I was a different woman too.

"Chairman, forgive me, but I wish that at some time years ago you could have told me about . . . all of this. I can't say how much it would have meant to me."

"There's a reason why I never could, Sayuri, and why I had to tell Mameha not to say anything, either. The reason is Nobu. There's something I want to discuss with you," he continued. "It's something Pumpkin said after she took me down to the theater on Amami. I was extremely angry with her, and I demanded to know why she'd done it. For a long time she wouldn't say anything. Then she told me something that made no sense at first. She said you'd asked her to bring Nobu."

"Chairman, please," I began unsteadily. "I made such a terrible mistake . . ."

"All right, Sayuri," he said. "Now you must understand my relationship with Nobu. Then it will be clear why I've treated you as I have over the years and it will also be clear why I've come here tonight."

And then the Chairman told me all the things I already knew from magazines; how Nobu saved Iwamura Electric in the 1920s, and how Nobu was like a brother to him.

"One day when I'd known you only a short time," he said, "Nobu brought you a present of a comb, and gave it to you in front of everyone at the party. That was when I realized how strong his feelings for you were. Well, I knew in a moment that I couldn't take away from him the thing he so clearly wanted."

"I like Nobu very much," I said, "but what I did on Amami . . . What I did on Amami, I did because of my feelings for you, Chairman. Every step I have taken in my life since I was a child in Gion, I have taken in the hope of bringing myself closer to you."

"Look at me, Sayuri."

I wanted to do as the Chairman asked, but I couldn't.

"When I saw you there with the Minister, you had a look in

your eyes just like the one I saw so many years ago at the Shirakawa Stream. You seemed so desperate, as if you might drown if someone didn't save you. After Pumpkin told me you had intended Nobu to see you with the Minister, I decided to tell him what I'd seen. And when he reacted so angrily . . . well, if Nobu couldn't forgive you for what you'd done, it was clear to me that he was never truly the man for you. Nobu has given you up, Sayuri. So I've taken nothing away from him."

I was still struggling to understand what was happening to me and what I ought to do or say when the Chairman pulled me close to him and kissed me.

It may surprise you to hear that this was the first time in my life that anyone had really kissed me. General Tottori had sometimes pressed his lips against mine when he was my *danna*, but there was so little love in it that I wondered if he just needed somewhere to rest his face.

Chapter 14   New York

Now, nearly forty years later, I sit here in New York and remember that evening with the Chairman as the moment when I finally stopped fighting against the stream of my life. It was also the end of my career as a geisha.

The reason is that the Chairman wanted to keep me away from Nobu, who now hated me. So he paid Mother a very large sum of money each month to let me stop work as a geisha.

The Chairman certainly wasn't going to marry me; he was already married. I still lived in the *okiya*, but I spent most of my time in a lovely house that the Chairman bought in the northeast of Kyoto. It was supposed to be for guests of Iwamura Electric, but the Chairman and I spent three or four evenings a week together there.

During the day I no longer went to geisha school or visited the teahouses, but I saw Mameha very often. We had tea together several times a week. After all she'd done for me since I was a child, and the special role she'd played in my relationship with the Chairman, I felt a debt to her that I could never repay.

I expected that this would be my life, entertaining the Chairman in the evening and occupying myself during the day in any way I could. But in the fall of 1952, I accompanied the Chairman on his second trip to the United States. It changed my life.

The Chairman said that on his previous visit to America he'd understood real wealth for the first time. Most Japanese at this time had electricity only during certain hours, for example, but the lights in American cities were on all the time. And even in small American towns, the Chairman told me, the movie theaters were as grand as our National Theater.

But he was most amazed by the fact that every family in the United States owned a refrigerator. This could be bought with an average worker's monthly salary. In Japan, a worker needed fifteen months' salary to buy such a thing; few families could afford it.

Then, when I looked out of the window of my room at the Waldorf-Astoria Hotel and saw buildings like mountains around me, and smooth, clean streets below, I had the feeling I was seeing a world in which anything was possible.

Over the next three years I traveled with the Chairman twice more to the United States. When he was out on business during the day, my maid and I went to museums and restaurants. We even found one of the few Japanese restaurants in New York. I'd known the manager well in Gion before the war.

During lunch one afternoon I found myself in a private room in the back of the restaurant, entertaining a number of men I hadn't seen in years—the Vice President of the Nippon Telephone Company, the new Japanese Ambassador, and a

Professor from Kyoto University. It was almost like being back in Gion again.

In the summer of 1956 the Chairman and I were sitting outdoors after dinner at Iwamura Electric's house in northeast Kyoto. The Chairman had just told me that he had a plan to open a branch of his company in New York. There was something I'd wanted to discuss with him for some time and this news gave me my chance.

"I keep thinking of the Ichiriki Teahouse," I began, "and truthfully, I'm beginning to realize how much I miss entertaining."

The Chairman just took a bite of his ice-cream and then put his spoon down on the dish again.

"Of course, I can never go back to work in Gion," I continued. "I know that perfectly well. But I wonder, *Danna-sama* . . . isn't there a place for a small teahouse in New York City?"

"I don't know what you're talking about," he said. "There's no reason why you should want to leave Japan."

"It's true that leaving Japan would be a big change. But now that *Danna-sama* will be spending more and more of his time in the United States . . ."

In August of that same year, I moved to New York City to start my own very small teahouse for Japanese businessmen and politicians traveling through the United States. Of course, Mother tried to make sure that my new business in New York would be controlled by the Nitta *okiya*, but the Chairman refused to consider any such arrangement.

Mother had power over me as long as I remained in Gion, but I broke my ties with her by leaving. The Chairman sent in two of his accountants to make sure that Mother gave me every last yen that I'd earned.

◆

New York is an exciting city. I felt at least as much at home as I ever did in Gion. In fact, as I look back, the many long weeks I've spent here with the Chairman have made my life in the United States even fuller and happier than it was in Japan.

My little teahouse, on the second floor of an old club off Fifth Avenue, was successful from the beginning. A number of geisha have come from Gion to work with me there, and even Mameha sometimes visits.

I never go back to Gion; I think I'd be disturbed by all the changes. After Mother's death, a few years ago, the Nitta *okiya* was pulled down and replaced by a bookshop with two apartments above it.

On his last visit to New York City, the Chairman and I took a walk through Central Park. He stood with his two weak, old hands on his walking stick, and his eyes closed, and he breathed in deeply the memories of the past.

"Sometimes," he sighed, "I think the things I remember are more real than the things I see."

We went back to my apartment and drank from each other until I was full of him and he was full of me. The Chairman died only a few months later.

Everything that ever happened to me was like a stream falling over rocks, down, down, until it reached the ocean—the Chairman. I've lived my life again just telling it to you.

It's true that when I cross Park Avenue, I notice how strange everything is. The yellow taxis that go rushing past, making that noise with their loud horns; the women in their business suits, who looked so surprised to see a little old Japanese woman standing on the street corner in a kimono. But, really, would Yoroido seem less strange if I went back there again?

Whatever our struggles, and whether we sink or swim, our world is no more permanent than a wave rising on the ocean.

ACTIVITIES

Translator's Note – Chapter 3

Before you read

1 Discuss these questions with another student.
   a When you think of Japanese life, culture, and traditions, what are the first five things that come into your head? Write them down and then compare your lists.
   b What do you know about geisha? What do they do?
2 Read the Introduction and answer these questions.
   a What do the following Japanese words mean?
      shamisen   tsutsumi   obi   takamakura   danna
   b Which of these would a geisha not do?
      dance for you   talk to you   kiss you   pour tea for you
      play music for you
3 Look at the Word List at the back of the book. Which are words:
   a for women?
   b usually for men?
   c for men and women?

While you read

4 In which order do these people speak to Chiyo (later known as Sayuri)? Number them 1–9.
   a Mrs. Nitta   .....
   b Mr. Bekku   .....
   c Asami   .....
   d Jakob Haarhuis   .....
   e Hatsumomo's lover   .....
   f the Chairman   .....
   g Pumpkin   .....
   h Tanaka Ichiro   .....
   i Mameha   .....

After you read

5 Answer these questions.

   a How are the people in Question 4 important in this part of the story?

   b What do you know about Hatsumomo?

6 Only one of these sentences is true. Correct the other sentences.

   a Nitta Sayuri uses her memoirs to get revenge on a few people who offended her.

   b Chiyo runs away to Kyoto, where she meets Hatsumomo.

   c Hatsumomo is friendly to Chiyo at first but becomes increasingly unpleasant.

   d Hatsumomo, Pumpkin, and Mr. Bekku live off the money that Mrs. Nitta earns.

   e Hatsumomo hits Chiyo across the face because Chiyo has been spying on her.

   f Mrs. Nitta forces Hatsumomo to pay for Mameha's ruined kimono.

   g Chiyo cries outside the Minamiza Theater because Hatsumomo has prevented her from training to be a geisha.

   h Hatsumomo is afraid that Mrs. Nitta might adopt Pumpkin as her daughter.

   i Mrs. Nitta and Hatsumomo have good reason to be unhappy about Mameha's plans for Chiyo.

7 Work with another student. Have this conversation between Chiyo's mother and father after Mr. Tanaka's visit.

   Student A: You are Chiyo's mother. You want Chiyo to go to Kyoto. Say why.

   Student B: You are Chiyo's father. You want Chiyo to stay in Yoroido. Say why.

8 Discuss these questions with another student.

   a Has anybody ever been jealous of you? Why? How did it make you feel about them?

   b What do the first three chapters tell you about life in Japan in the 1930s?

   c Would life as a geisha be considered a respectable profession for a girl today in your country? Why (not)?

Chapters 4–6

Before you read

9 In the last chapter, Hatsumomo tells Mameha, "If you think you can make Chiyo into a more successful geisha than Pumpkin, you can expect a big surprise." What might this surprise be?

While you read

10 Finish these sentences. Write one name or word in each space.
   a Chiyo learns to play the .... and the ....
   b .... and .... stop talking to each other.
   c A novice geisha has to sleep on a .... after having her .... done.
   d Mameha teaches Chiyo to make a man .... with her ....
   e At the Ichiriki Teahouse, Chiyo becomes a .... geisha and has her name changed to ....
   f Hatsumomo pays .... to telephone her whenever Sayuri and Mameha visit a first-class ....
   g If Mrs. Nitta .... Pumpkin, ... is safe.
   h Mameha wants .... men to bid against each other for Sayuri's ....
   i Sayuri usually keeps the Chairman's .... in the .... of her kimono.
   j Nobu has terrible .... on his face and only one ....

After you read

11 How does Chiyo / Sayuri feel, and why,
   a about the smell of roasted tea leaves?
   b after Hatsumomo pulls Pumpkin's lip?
   c about the preparations for the ceremony to make her a novice geisha?
   d about geisha parties in general?
   e before, during, and after Naga Teruomi's party?
   f in a luxury car south of the city?
   g a few days after her conversation with Mameha on Shijo Avenue Bridge?

h about Nobu Toshikazu?

i when she pours tea for the Chairman?

j after the *sumo* exhibition?

12 Discuss these statements with another student. Do you agree with them? Why (not)?

a "Hatsumomo is a more successful Older Sister than Mameha."

b "Sayuri would be happier if she stopped thinking about the Chairman."

c "Mameha and Sayuri are too easily frightened."

13 Work with another student. Have this conversation between Mrs. Nitta and Mameha.

Student A: You are Mrs. Nitta. You plan to adopt Pumpkin. Tell Mameha why.

Student B: You are Mameha. You think that Mrs. Nitta should adopt Sayuri. Tell her why.

Chapters 7–9

Before you read

14 Why might Hatsumomo still try to cause trouble for Sayuri? How might she do this? Will she be successful, do you think? Why (not)?

While you read

15 Tick (✓) the correct answer.

a Sayuri thinks that

    1) Nobu will win the bid for her *mizuage*. .....

    2) a *mizuage* with Nobu will destroy her hopes. .....

b After the Iwamura Electric party, Sayuri feels

    1) victorious. .....

    2) embarrassed. .....

c Dr. Crab is annoyed with Sayuri because

    1) Nobu has given her a gift. .....

    2) Hatsumomo has told him lies about her. .....

d After Sayuri's *mizuage*,

    1) Hatsumomo and Sayuri become friendlier. .....

    2) Dr. Crab loses interest in Sayuri. .....

e Sayuri does not want Nobu to be her *danna* because she

    1) values her independence. .....

    2) prefers another man. .....

f Mrs. Nitta finally agrees that

    1) Nobu will be a better *danna* than General Tottori. .....

    2) General Tottori will be a better *danna* than Nobu. .....

g After Sayuri moves into her room, Hatsumomo physically attacks

    1) Mameha. .....

    2) an old friend. .....

h Hatsumomo leaves the *okiya* because she

    1) is jealous of Sayuri. .....

    2) has no choice. .....

After you read

16 Who says these words, who to, and why?

    a "Isn't she the loveliest creature."

    b "She told the Doctor that you have a boyfriend."

    c "I think less of you for introducing this girl to me."

    d "One day the *okiya* will be yours."

    e "She told me something very strange."

    f "That is something you're in no position to ask for."

    g "The time has come for you to exchange rooms with them."

    h "I never try to defeat the man I'm fighting."

    i "She really does seem to be losing her mind."

    j "As a favor to me ... *do* try to calm down."

17 Work with another student. You are making the seating arrangements for the following eight people at a dinner party. The table is round, and everybody must sit between people who will be friendly to them. Where should each person sit, and why?

Dr. Crab   Nobu Toshikazu   Mrs. Nitta   Hatsumomo

Pumpkin   General Tottori   Bando Shojiro   Sayuri

18 Discuss these questions with another student.

    a Do you feel sorry for Nobu Toshikazu? Why (not)?

    b Do you approve of Mameha's treatment of Hatsumomo in Chapter 9? Why (not)?

c Does Hatsumomo deserve to be thrown out of the *okiya*? Why (not)?

Chapters 10–12

Before you read

19 What problems might World War II create for Sayuri and the other geisha in Kyoto?

While you read

20 Who or what are these sentences about?
    a In Japan it is referred to as *kuraitani*. ....
    b The government closes it. ....
    c Sayuri makes them during the war. ....
    d She grows richer during the war. ....
    e He is sick in the snow. ....
    f She is popular with the Americans. ....
    g They both want to be Sayuri's *danna*. ....
    and ....
    h Sayuri betrays him. ....
    i They see Sayuri alone with Sato. ....
    and ....

After you read

21 How are these places important in this part of the story?
    a the registry office   **f** Nagasaki
    b the Suruya Inn   **g** the Gion Shrine
    c the Ichiriki Teahouse   **h** the Hanami-cho area of Gion
    d the country outside Kyoto   **i** the island of Amami
    e the Kamo River   **j** an old theater

22 Answer these questions.
How:
    a does Nobu help Sayuri during the war?
    b does Pumpkin survive the war?
Why:
    c doesn't Sayuri ask the Chairman or Nobu for help when she hears that Gion is closing?
    d does Nobu want Sayuri to entertain Sato?

What:

e disappoints Sayuri at the *okiya* in the Hanami-cho area of Gion?

f makes Sayuri feel foolish at the Ichiriki Teahouse?

On the island of Amami, why does:

g Sayuri want to betray Nobu?

h Sayuri want to be alone with Sato?

i Pumpkin take the Chairman to the theater?

23 Discuss these statements with another student. Do you agree with them? Why (not)?

a "Sayuri should feel ashamed of her behavior."

b "The Chairman does not deserve to keep his company."

Chapters 13–14

Before you read

24 Will the story end happily or unhappily for these people, do you think? Why?

a Sayuri

b Nobu

c the Chairman

While you read

25 Are these sentences true (✓) or false (✗)?

a Pumpkin has accidentally betrayed Sayuri. .....

b Sayuri briefly considers killing herself. .....

c Sayuri is prepared to have Nobu as her *danna*. .....

d The Chairman is surprised that Sayuri remembers him from the time when she was only a maid. .....

e Without the Chairman's help, Sayuri would never have become a geisha. .....

f Nobu has lost interest in Sayuri after the events on the island of Amami. .....

g The Chairman wants Sayuri to live in America with him. .....

h Sayuri continues to work for Mrs. Nitta after she moves to New York.

After she moves to New York, Sayuri never meets
any of her old friends from Kyoto again. .....

j Sayuri continues to wear traditional Japanese clothes
when she is an old woman in New York. .....

After you read

26 Think about your answers to Question 24 again. Were you right?

27 Find the endings to these statements about Sayuri, below.

a She is embarrassed and afraid because she

b She is confused and upset because she

c She feels relief at the inn because she

d She does not throw the handkerchief in the sea because she

e She feels grateful to the Chairman because he

f She feels relief at the Ichiriki Teahouse because she

g The Chairman has never spoken truthfully to her before because
he

h The Chairman can express his love for her because Nobu

i She annoys Mrs. Nitta because she

j She feels calm as she gets older because she

1) remembers earlier words of advice.

2) never wants to see her again.

3) avoids embarrassing conversations.

4) wanted to avoid hurting a friend.

5) starts a new business in New York.

6) is angrily criticized by Pumpkin.

7) has an unexpected visitor.

8) knows that the events in her life have been inevitable.

9) once had a secret conversation with Mameha.

10) was seen at the theater by the wrong person.

28 Discuss these statements with another student. Do you agree with
them? Why (not)?

a "Pumpkin is right to feel angry with Sayuri."

b "Hatsumomo is the most interesting character in this book."

c "Women would like this book more than men."

Writing

29 Write an account of the events at the Shirakawa Stream (Chapter 3) from the Chairman's point of view.

30 Imagine that you are Chiyo (Chapter 3). Write a letter to Mr. Tanaka in Yoroido about your first two years in the Nitta *okiya*. Do you want to stay in Kyoto or do you want to return home? Why?

31 Imagine that you are Sayuri (Chapter 5). Write a letter of complaint to Mrs. Nitta about Hatsumomo's unfair treatment of you since you first arrived at the *okiya*.

32 Write about the importance of two of these people in the story. How might Sayuri's life have been different without them?
Dr. Crab, General Tottori, Sato, Pumpkin

33 What happens to Hatsumomo after she leaves the Nitta *okiya* (Chapter 10)? Write her story.

34 Imagine that you are Nobu Toshikazu (Chapter 12). You want to be Sayuri's *danna*. Write a letter to her, explaining why you think that you are the perfect man for her.

35 Imagine that you are Sayuri (Chapter 13). Write a letter to Nobu Toshikazu. Ask him to forgive you for your unkind treatment of him and explain why you acted the way you did.

36 Imagine that you are Mrs. Nitta, after Sayuri has gone to New York (Chapter 13). You are looking for another girl to train as a geisha. Write an advertisement for a Kyoto newspaper. How could a young girl benefit from training to be a geisha? What rewards would this career bring her in later life?

37 Imagine that you are Sayuri. Mameha once told you, "We don't become geisha because we want our lives to be happy; we become geisha because we have no choice." Write a letter to a young girl who wants to be a geisha. Advise her against it, using your own experience and Mameha's words to support your opinion.

38 "Mrs. Nitta is a good businesswoman but a bad human being." Do you agree with this statement? Why (not)? Write about her.

Answers for the Activities in this book are available from the Pearson English Readers website. A free Activity Worksheet is also available from the website. Activity worksheets are part of the Pearson English Readers Teacher Support Programme, which also includes Progress tests and Graded Reader Guidelines. For more information, please visit: www.pearsonenglishreaders.com

Better learning
comes from fun.

Pearson English **Readers**

There are plenty of Pearson English Readers to choose from
- world classics, film and television adaptations, short stories, thrillers,
modern-day crime and adventure, biographies, American classics,
non-fiction, plays ... and more to come.

For a complete list of all Pearson English Readers titles, please contact
your local Pearson Education office or visit the website.

pearsonenglishreaders.com

Notes:

Notes:

WORD LIST

admiral (n) a high-ranking officer in the navy

apprentice (n) someone who works for an employer for a fixed period of time to learn a job or skill

baron (n) the title of an upper-class man

cabaret (n) entertainment, usually with songs and music, performed in a restaurant or club while customers eat and drink

cherry (n) a small, round, red fruit with a stone in the middle

courtyard (n) an open space that is completely or partly surrounded by buildings

crab (n) a sea creature with a hard shell and five legs on each side; the flesh of a crab can be eaten

engagement (n) an arrangement to do something

fan (n) a flat object that you wave with your hand to make yourself feel cooler

futon (n) a large, thick pad filled with soft material that is used for sleeping on, especially in Japan

geisha (n) a Japanese woman who is trained in the art of dancing, singing, and providing entertainment, especially for men

grunt (n/v) to make short, low sounds in your throat, especially when you do not want to talk

inn (n) a small hotel, especially one in the countryside

kimono (n) a traditional piece of Japanese clothing, like a long, loose coat with wide sleeves

maid (n) a female servant

mat (n) a piece of thick material that covers part of a floor. **Tatami mats**, made of dried plants, are a traditional Japanese floor covering.

memoirs (n pl) a book, usually by someone important and famous, about his or her life and experiences

mistress (n) a woman who owns or controls a place

novice (n) someone who has no experience in a skill or activity

parachute (n) a piece of equipment used by people who jump out of planes to help them fall slowly and safely to the ground

peasant (n) a poor farmer who owns or rents a small amount of land

prime minister (n) the most important minister and leader of the government in many countries that have a parliament

rickshaw (n) a small vehicle used in Asia for carrying one or two passengers and pulled by someone walking (as in Japan, in the past) or riding a bicycle

shrine (n) a place, often connected with a holy person or event, where people go to pray

stump (n) the short part of an arm or leg that remains after the rest of it has been cut off

sumo wrestling (n) a Japanese contact sport in which two large fighters try to force each other out of a circular area or to touch the ground with any part of the body except the bottoms of their feet

talcum powder (n) a pleasant-smelling powder that you put on your body after washing

terrify (v) to make someone extremely afraid

turning point (n) the time when an important change begins, especially one that improves the situation

yen (n) a unit of Japanese money

Made in the USA
Columbia, SC
20 July 2024

38991777R00067